I NEVER MEANT
TO MAKE YOU CRY

By

Loretta Heard

ISBN: 1-4107-5012-4 (e-book)
ISBN: 1-4107-5343-3 (Paperback)

This book is printed on acid-free paper.

1stBooks – rev. 07/18/03

Dedication

This book is dedicated to the memory of my deceased father,

Deacon Lessie Heard

Acknowledgments

First, I want to thank God for being in my life; with Him all things are possible.

Heartfelt gratitude to my mom Thelma Heard, for her unconditional love, prayers and faith in me. To my son Courtney, thanks for your patience. Special thank you to my sister Janice. I couldn't have written this book without you. To my family and friends who encouraged and believed in me. Very special thanks to my good friends Elaine, Lorraine, Louise and Orrin for being you.

God truly blessed me with love.

Peace

Set me as a seal upon your heart

As a seal upon your arm

For love is as strong as death.

Song of Solomon 8:6

"Code Red, Code Red!" How I remember these words so clearly in my mind. A waiting room full of hope turned into a moment of disbelief. The doctor approached my family with the most shocking words I had ever experienced. "We lost him; he's no longer breathing." I sat there unable to comprehend the words that came through his mouth. I was numb at the words that I heard, and didn't want to believe that my father was dead. Gone, finished, never to speak again. I was devastated. The core, the rock that held our family together was now a missing link.

Robin was the second of five siblings. She knew that the task ahead would be very difficult. How would she mirror all that her father stood for? For she knew she'd be the one to fill his shoes. Robin knew that she had to hide her emotions, bury them deep within to hold the family together. Holding back tears, she embraced her mom who let out a loud scream which could be heard through the closed doors. Robin held her mom tight, felt her trembling body, and knew that there was nothing she could say or do to take away the pain. Robin, tried so hard to keep her faith in God, knowing this was one of the values taught and instilled in her by her parents. She fought a feeling of despair, wondering *why*? Why would God allow so much pain? Why would he take away the one man whom she loved in the entire world? *Why is my Daddy gone?* she wondered.

Westchester

September 4th -- six years ago to the day. Robin reached over to turn off the alarm clock to start her workday. The anniversary of her dad's death was the first thing on her mind. She held her stomach, feeling the pain as if it were yesterday, so vividly in her mind she could recall that day in the hospital waiting room when she heard those words, "He's gone."

She made her way to the bathroom with tears rolling down her face. *I'm not going to be sad today-- this is the day that the Lord has made. I'm to rejoice and be glad in it.* But oh, how she longed to just hear her daddy's voice! She pulled herself together, washed her face, looked at herself in the mirror and decided that this day was going to be a happy not sad day. *I'm going to think on the good times we had with Dad, and rejoice in that.* Off to work she went.

Robin pulled into the parking lot; she arrived at the same time her girl Raine did. Robin, reading the expression on her girlfriend's face, knew how much they both hated their jobs at the factory.

"Twelve long hours," Raine said. "I don't feel like this today."

Robin, feeling it, too, said to herself, *It's 4 a.m.; even the birds aren't out of bed. I don't feel like doing this either.*

Raine knew from the expression on Robin's face that there was something wrong, something other than coming to work. Raine was a close friend, one who didn't hold back on what she felt. She was tough on the exterior, but soft on the inside.

"Are you all right, Robin?" Raine asked.

"This is going to be one long day," Robin replied.

Robin had always been good at masking her feelings. Deep down inside she knew that was half the reason why she had married Fred. Thinking back on that mistake, she now realized she had tried to escape her hurt over her Dad's death by seeking love -- someone to rescue her from the pain. What a nightmare! All her life, from the time she was a little girl, she had longed for a beautiful wedding. God granted her that wish, but to the wrong man. Robin met Fred soon after her Dad's death.

Fred had none of the qualifications Robin sought in a mate, qualities that her dad had displayed. Robin's belief was that a man was supposed to be the head of his house, the provider, the man in every respect of the word. Fred had a sense of humor and made Robin laugh; often she could forget her hurt, the pain which she had buried inside after her dad's death.

Fred was tall, slim and attractive in his own way. Physically there was no attraction on Robin's part, but she saw great potential in Fred. Fred was a jack-of-all-trades and could fix anything with his hands. It was a God-given talent, which came very naturally to him. Robin looked at the talent he possessed and felt the need to nurture him, bring out the best in this person who seemed lost. She needed a sense of purpose, someone to build up; little did she know this was a road to destruction.

When she first laid eyes on Fred, his appearance was that of a homeless person, someone who didn't believe in himself. Fred seemed to keep up with his hygiene, but the rest of him was torn up.

4

He had an innocence about him that made it possible for Robin to look beyond his outward appearance. He made her laugh. Robin, living at home with her mom, felt a great pressure and responsibility in helping her mother maintain the house. Robin felt overwhelmed at times. She felt responsible for her mom; someone had to be strong for her, after all, she was grieving after 35 years of marriage.

Everything that could go wrong with the house after dad's death did go wrong. There was a terrible flood in the basement, and Robin, not knowing who to call, knew that she'd better take on the responsibility and get it fixed. This was her very first encounter with Fred. He had been introduced to Robin by an associate. She called him to see if he could fix the problem, and indeed Fred did save the day. Robin began to see Fred on the regular and because of his sense of humor, she took a liking to him. He was her safety net, her way out of a dark and grieving pain.

Robin encouraged Fred to get his appearance in order, to feel good about himself, to be grateful for the gift that God had given him and allow that gift to bless him. They began seeing each other every day. It was a friendship, each one feeding off the other's weakness for their own strengths.

Fred had his own apartment. He was always a gentleman, never stepping out of place with Robin. She could see the excitement in his face whenever she was in his presence. She began to see that he was beginning to feel good about himself. Since Fred lived within a short distance from her job, every day after work Robin stopped by to see him.

Fred was unemployed but looking for a job. He claimed he made his money by using his handyman skills. Robin kept Fred a secret from her girlfriends because she didn't want anyone to know that she was seeing Fred on the regular. Robin even kept Fred from her best friend Ellen, whom she shared her deepest feelings with. Ellen was spiritual-minded and accepted a person for who they were. Robin and Ellen had a special kind of closeness, like sisters so Robin knew that she had to give in to her secret about Fred and eventually tell Ellen. Robin and Ellen had always talked about family, that special someone, and how they both wanted that for each other. Robin knew that if anyone would understand the relationship she had with Fred it would be Ellen.

Robin had just finished a long 12-hour shift and was looking forward to paying a visit to Fred. Fred didn't have a phone, so she always dropped in unexpectedly. He often looked forward to her coming. Fred was hilarious; he'd say the craziest thing just to make Robin laugh, and that was the highlight of her day. Often when she visited they'd sit outside the brick apartment building. She wondered why he'd never invite her in, but it wasn't a big deal; she enjoyed his company. This particular day he wasn't outside waiting for her.

Robin figured he'd gotten busy doing a job so she would stop by tomorrow. Instead she decided to pay a visit to Ellen -- now would be a good time to tell Ellen about Fred.

"Ellen, he's not anyone I would romantically involve myself with, but we've been spending a lot of time together. Girl, let me know if you need anything fixed because he's good with his hands."

Ellen was glad that Robin had met a new friend who kept her laughing.

Robin, not looking for anyone in a romantic sense, had just been going along day to day praying that one day she'd stumble into Mr. Right. Besides, her long-lost love was Gerald. How much she adored him! Gerald was tall, black, and handsome and had a smile that could win any woman over. He was quite a catch; the only problem was he was married. Robin knew that he was off-limits, but her heart ached for him. Gerald ached for her, too.

He had a passion for Robin, but also knew that it was wrong to cross the line. There was no denying that when they were in each other's presence they both felt it. The attraction drew them like a magnet. Robin would keep her distance, because she knew she would be weak when it came to resisting the temptation of Gerald. He had her spellbound. She loved Gerald with every fiber of her being.

Robin imagined what it would be like waking up to him every morning, spending her life with him, her true love. Robin knew that was one dream or fantasy that would never become a reality. Gerald was loyal in every sense of the word, and this made her adore him more. Robin and Gerald had a special bond with one another, but they knew they couldn't do anything about it. They had been intimate one time long before he was married. That one night of passion had nothing to do with the love she felt for him; it was love at first sight. The one night of desire just opened her heart more. Robin never loved any other man the way she felt for Gerald, but Gerald had unsettling issues with the woman he had married and didn't want to inflict any hurt upon Robin. Gerald explained to Robin that he would always love her in his own way, but they could never be more than friends.

Robin's shattered heart knew that she could never ever love anyone as much. She stopped the clock, put love on hold, promising to love this man until her dying day. Robin would never forget the day they said good-bye to love, but hello to a beautiful friendship.

Robin often remembered the times she'd cry on Sydney's shoulders about Gerald. Sydney was twice her age and the father of her child. He wore many hats, not only as the father of her child, but he was like a father, friend and companion to Robin. She was able to be herself with Sydney. Sydney had a deep love for Robin, but he knew that the age difference between them just didn't work.

Sydney was so thankful for their child. Robin's bearing him a son gave him a new lease on life. He was a great father to Larry. They were inseparable. Robin had no worries when it came to Sydney being a responsible father. Larry never wanted for anything.

Sydney was a character. He was very distinguished for his age. If he liked you, he'd do anything in the world for you; if he didn't care for you, he didn't see the sense in wasting either your time or his. Sydney and Robin both accepted each other for who they were and realized their bond was special. Sydney adored Robin, thought she was the prettiest black woman he had ever laid eyes on, but he knew that he could never fill all of her heart's desires of one day having a husband. Still, he felt a need to always care for her.

Robin never took advantage of Sydney's kindness; she loved him in her own way and always looked after him. Larry never wanted for anything; if Sydney could get it for him he would. Robin felt very blessed to have had a man of his character for her son's father and to be his best friend.

"Raine," she said now, "we've got six hours more to go. Girl, these 12-hour days are killing me."

Robin knew she'd be going to visit Fred after work. She drove up in front of his apartment building. Since this time Fred wasn't on the steps, she decided to ring the bell. After she'd rung it several times, he finally came to the door. Robin knew from the look on his face that something was different. He had shaved all the hair off his face, had gotten a clean cut. When she first met him, he had looked like a walking cave man. Robin was impressed.

Although the look was impressive, Fred was acting different. He acted as though he had been drinking. His speech was slurred, and he didn't seem so innocent. Robin thought it would be best if she left.

Fred grabbed her arm as she walked to her car and said to her, "Woman, you're the one for me, the one I prayed for, the one who'll marry me."

Robin got into her car and took off in disbelief. She had never seen that bold side of Fred, but then she realized that she kind of liked it. Driving home gave Robin time to collect her thought, and she decided not to drop in on Fred unexpectedly again. Turning in to her driveway, she knew what coming home meant. She'd have to face her grieving mom, her face filled with sorrow and hurt.

She went inside to get ready for the next long day. Mom seemed so lost, nothing but grief eating at her. As much as Robin hated her long 12-hour workdays, she would rather be at work than watch the pain in her mom's face.

Raine had a way of sensing when something was on Robin's mind. The next morning on the job she said, "Robin, what's up with you today? You seem so preoccupied in thought."

Robin had been thinking of the day before, and the difference she had seen in Fred. Wondering when she'd see him again, Robin said she just had some things on her mind, nothing to worry about. Robin felt that she wasn't ready to tell Raine about her new friend. Ellen would understand; Raine would say, "Why waste your time on someone who doesn't have a job?"

Raine was sensitive to certain things, but when it came to a man she had no sympathy at all. Raine had a mate, one she had been with for years, and he was good to and for her. She wanted the best for Robin, and nothing less than that. Anything that appeared to have a flaw she had nothing good to say about.

Another long day was over. When it was time to leave work, the place was like a racetrack, with everyone racing to see who would leave the lot first. Raine noticed a note on the windshield of Robin's car. Robin grabbed the note, which read, "I'm sorry about yesterday. Please stop by." It was a note from Fred. Trying to hide it from Raine, Robin stuck it in her bag.

Raine said, "What was that, some secret admirer? Girl, don't involve yourself with no one around here; it's not worth your time."

Robin went straight to Fred's apartment. He was sitting on the steps waiting. As always, he greeted her with his humor and said, "It's a big world out there, and I just happened to have you."

Robin looked surprised, because she then realized Fred had taken a liking to her. Fred had made dinner for Robin, and this was the first time he invited her inside. She didn't want to hurt his feelings by declining the dinner invitation so Robin went inside with hesitation. She was not afraid of Fred in any way, but she felt uncomfortable.

The apartment was shabby; none of the décor was modern or even new. It was a very small studio with a couch bed, table and a small black and white TV. Still, although the apartment didn't have much and had very little décor, it was very clean. Robin realized how blessed she was to have so much. She told Fred she'd take a rain check on the dinner, since she'd had a big lunch.

Fred was shy; he had explained to Robin that he had been married before, but was now divorced. He also told her that in his entire life he had only been intimate with two women. Fred was 43 years old. Robin couldn't believe her ears. In a lot of ways, Fred acted like a scared little boy, almost as if he'd never grown up, a boy in a man's body. He seemed very naive when it came to the opposite sex.

Fred said he came from a family of eight kids. It was obvious he didn't have fatherly guidance. Fred told Robin he had had to work for everything. He had nothing given to him by his parents. He told Robin that he had hurt his back on the last job and, due to permanent injuries, he was on disability compensation. This was his only means of support, which wasn't very much a month. He used his talents to pick up odd jobs and make extra money to survive.

Robin accepted Fred for who he was and didn't look down on him for having less. She was glad he was able to open up to her to talk about the things that had happened in his life.

It was Christmas. Three months had passed since Robin and Fred had met. He was so excited, like a kid in a candy store, with Robin helping him decorate the apartment. Robin couldn't believe she was out in such bad weather. There was a blizzard, and she was worried about getting home. Fred asked her to stay the night; otherwise he'd be worried about her safety. The weather advisory flashed on the TV screen every five minutes. Robin had no choice but to stay; she was snowed in for the night. Fred didn't have a phone, and she was worried about letting her mom know she was safe. She didn't want to upset her mom since she had enough to deal with.

Fred suggested he ask his neighbor if it would be all right to use his phone. Robin called home to tell her mom she was staying over with a friend, and that she'd be home first thing in the morning when the roads cleared. Robin then called Sydney to make sure Larry was OK. Sydney took good care of their son, and she never had to worry when Larry was in his care.

Fred only had the fold-out couch, and Robin was wondering where she would sleep. Fred was a bit uneasy, and he explained that he had never had a woman stay overnight before, especially one as pretty as Robin. He reassured her that she'd be safe and that she could sleep in the fold-out bed; he'd sleep on the floor.

They hung the Christmas lights in the window and stayed up half the night just talking. Robin fell off to sleep and, before she knew it, the sun was shining on her face. When she awoke, Fred was sitting in one spot just staring at her. Robin asked him if something was wrong. He said "You're just so beautiful."

Robin thought, *What a way to start the day!* She smiled. Fred said he hadn't slept at all.

"I looked at you half the night," he said. "I watched you sleep."

The storm was over. Robin made her way home, all the while thinking about how she had stayed the entire night with Fred and he hadn't made one sexual attempt, not even to kiss her or touch her in bed. She thought that made him an exceptional man. It just made her wonder about him.

Robin had a nice weekend. She spent Saturday with Larry and Sydney in the park. Robin knew that Larry loved her, but she couldn't compete with the bond that he and Sydney shared. Larry spent most of his time with his dad.

Sydney had a gangster mentality and taught Larry at a very young age to shoot a gun. Although he did teach him the safety of a gun, Robin felt that her baby was too young to be experienced with a gun. Sydney bought Larry his first hunting rifle at the age of seven. Robin was beside herself. She couldn't understand how Sydney thought bringing their son to the woods would later prevent him from hanging in the streets. Larry had a passion for hunting, just like his dad. He'd rather sleep in the woods than eat when he was hungry.

Larry had always been in church from the time he was a baby. Robin had been reared in the church, and that was one of the values she instilled in her son, just as her parents did with her.

The Family

Since her dad's death, the family had never seemed able to connect when it came to family gatherings. Now it was Christmas time, a time for love, family and togetherness. The absence of Robin's dad put a distance between family members. Robin knew how much it meant to her mom to have everyone together.

She could remember her childhood Christmas years; she had always been grateful for what Santa left under the tree. Dad, always at the head of the table, had blessed the meal which mom had prepared days in advance. The family had always been so thankful to God for the blessings that were given. Robin, as the second eldest of five children, had tried to make the spirit live on. She was determined to have the family together for Christmas dinner.

Everyone had his or her own agenda and their own unique personalities. Lamont was the eldest and the only boy. He was spoiled by all the girls and had always considered himself to be the black sheep. Lamont had a drug problem, though he never blamed anyone else for the choices he made or the road he chose in life. Still, he was always looking to his family for help, in and out of jail, always making that his second place of dwelling. Somehow Mom felt secure knowing when he was in jail.

Janet, the middle child, was always busy. A real super mom. Her focus was on her job, kids and mate. She was close but kept a safe distance from the family. You could count on Janet; she'd be there when she had to be.

Karen was next to youngest; she carried a few extra pounds and was always self-conscious about her weight. Karen was very outgoing, always a people person...if she liked you. She had a voice for singing. She could sing like an angel, but she lacked self-esteem; because of her size, she always found excuses not to be present at family gatherings.

Tutie was the baby; she was wild, young and crazy. Tutie was the family comedienne. She never took anything seriously.

Janet and Robin were the two best cooks. Tutie couldn't boil water. Being the baby, she had never had to cook. Mom had been working when everyone lived at home; she worked the second shift so she'd taught Janet and Robin to fix the meals when she was too tired. Everyone had a job to do around the house because of Mom's work schedule, Dad made sure the girls kept the house in order.

Robin knew if she was to pull this gathering off successfully she'd better contact Janet. Besides, she didn't want to put the burden on her mom; it was too much. It was time for her mother to relax and let the girls do for her.

Robin called all the sisters. "Janet, we're all meeting at Mom's for Christmas dinner. What can you bring?"

Janet said, "My money is tight; if you buy the food, I'll cook it."

Robin knew that was coming. Janet was always penny-pinching. She'd contribute, but it was like pulling pearls out the sea.

"OK, Janet," Robin said. "I'll bring the money by there tomorrow; you buy what you need."

She called Karen next. "Hi, Karen, I'm planning Christmas dinner for us at Mom's. What can you bring?"

Karen said, "Robin, you know I'm not cooking."

Robin knew that was out of the question. Karen started naming foods she wanted on the menu. "Yeah, don't forget the yellow rice, turkey, ham and green beans…"

Robin thought *What nerve!* "What the hell are you going to bring, since you've got the menu in order?"

Karen said, "I'll bring paper plates and napkins."

Robin didn't get an attitude, because she knew what to expect from Karen, and she figured anything was better than nothing.

She called Tutie last. "Tutie, Christmas dinner is at Mom's. What are you bringing?"

Tutie said, "I'll pick up the soda and alcoholic beverages."

Robin said, "Tutie, do you think you can at least read the directions on the back of a box of cake and figure out how to make it?"

"Robin, don't play with me," Tutie said sharply. "What kind of cake? I don't have a cake pan; what should I bake it in?"

By now Robin's nerves were spent; she hung up the phone.

Robin didn't bother to contact Lamont. His being there alone would be a miracle. This was the first Christmas she'd known him not to be in jail. She told Tutie to get in touch with him, let him know what time, and tell him to please show up.

Robin said, "Momma, I've set the table, the Christmas music is playing, and everyone will be here soon. Don't worry, there's more than enough food."

Her mom said, "You know your sister Janet; she won't cook enough food to say grace over."

Robin had been slaving over the stove for days. Now she said "Mom, don't worry, everything will be fine, and we'll all be together."

All Mom's kids were there and all the grandkids. She was happy but still there was sadness. Kevin, the oldest grandchild, had four kids; he was Lamont's only child. Janet had three kids, Niki, Deon and Lenna. Karen's two girls were Tracy and Jasmine. Tutie's three were Jackie, Kim and Mike. Robin's son Larry was there, too. Mom loved when all her grandkids were present. She said it made her feel old, being a great-grandma.

Tracy, Karen's eldest daughter, was always a smart-mouth. She and her mom were always at odds because they were so much alike. Tracy and her Aunt Tutie were always at each other. They'd argue over the stupidest thing, and then they'd laugh and make up as if they'd never had words. Robin thought her family was very dysfunctional, but it all boiled down to them loving one another in their own way.

Mom began the grace. "Bow your heads, and let's give thanks to God. Thank You, Lord, for my family being together. Amen!"

Mom was sitting at the head of the table, the place where Dad had always sat. She said grace with a tremor in her voice. It was a tradition for the family to always give honor for the food they were so thankful to have.

Everyone was getting their grub on; it was very quiet at the table. Robin sensed that everybody was feeling the same thing, missing Dad. Tutie started talking in her baby language. She was a clown who rubbed Tracy the wrong way; before you knew it Tracy and her Aunt Tutie were arguing. Things were back to normal. Tracy resembled Robin. She didn't lack anything in the self-esteem department; she'd always say "I look good and so does my family."

Organizing dinner had been tough, but Robin managed it. The family was together, everybody under the same roof, and that pleased her mom.

Robin asked, "Who's doing the dishes?"

"Mom, can I take a potato pie?" Karen said. "I'm sick and ready to go home."

After getting her belly full, she decided to get sick. Robin smiled because everyone was acting like old times. Janet, always the first to exit with half the leftovers, everything except the kitchen sink, never wanting to contribute but never left empty-handed, made her exit first with her family.

Everyone had gone home. Robin did last minute touch-ups and asked, "Ma, did you have a good time?"

Her mom said, "Baby, it was wonderful, all my kids being with me, especially Lamont. Thank You, Lord, all went well."

Robin said, "Good night, Ma."

"Good night, Robin," her mother replied, "and thanks. Your Dad would be proud."

Robin wrapped up a plate for Sydney. He was a part of the family, but didn't like gatherings. He'd rather stay in and watch his baseball game. She also put a plate aside for Fred, figuring she'd bring it to him after work tomorrow.

Robin was exhausted and ready to call it a night; she waited for Sydney to pick up Larry. *Let me make sure the door is locked, then I'm down for the count*, she thought. She said her prayers and to bed she went.

Westchester

Mornings came so quick; the phone rang. Robin wondered who could be calling so early, it was 3:00 a.m. It was her friend Ellen.

"Hello, Robin? I'm sorry to call so early. I hope I didn't wake your Mom. My car won't start. Can you give me a ride to work?"

Robin said, "Sure, Ellen, not a problem. I'll be there in the next 30 minutes."

When she got there, Ellen said, "Hey, girl thanks for picking me up. How are things with your new friend Fred?"

Robin said, "Ellen, I stayed over the night of that bad blizzard, and he did not make one pass at me."

Ellen said, "Girl, is he gay? Is he a man, or what?"

They both laughed. Robin said, "Not that I wanted him to, but it was nice to be in the presence of a gentleman."

When they arrived in the parking lot, Raine pulled up beside them.

Robin whispered to Ellen, "Promise not to say anything to Raine yet about Fred. I want to be the first to tell her."

"I promise," Ellen said.

"What's up? You all ready to do the long day?" Raine said. "I hate this place; there's got to be a better way. These hours are way too long and it's burning my nerves out."

"Maybe we can get lucky and find a rich guy," Ellen laughed sarcastically.

Raine said, "Stop trippin'. It's too damn early; let's just do this."

Raine was tough, but she was a real sweetheart, too. She was very selective in her choice of friends. She liked Robin a lot and would always tell it like it is.

At the end of their shift, Robin said, "Raine, we'll see you in the morning. I'm going to take Ellen on home. I'll give you a buzz in the morning to wake you." They had a buddy system with the phones just in case they overslept.

Ellen said, "Robin, aren't you going to go by to see your friend Fred?"

Robin said, "I figured I'd drop you off first. Don't worry, Ellen, you'll meet him in time."

Ellen said, "Call me in the morning, girl, to wake me up. Have a good time over Fred's. See you tomorrow."

Robin, running behind schedule, arrived at Fred's later than usual. She hated that he didn't have a phone. She didn't know if he would still be waiting on the steps or not. *I'll just ride by and take my chances. I want him to have this plate of food.*

Robin pulled up in front of the building, and sure enough, he was there. He greeted her with a big smile.

"I thought you had forgotten about me. I've waited for you all my life…I mean…an hour!" Fred joked.

Robin explained to him that her girlfriend's car wasn't working, and she'd had to take her home.

"What's wrong with her car? I fix cars, too. You break it, I fix it," Fred said.

Robin said, "I have no idea what's wrong, but I'll be sure to pass that information on to my friend."

Robin thought it was her imagination at first, but she was sure she smelled alcohol. She said, "Fred, have you been drinking?"

Fred answered, "I drank a beer or two to quench my thirst."

Robin asked, "Do you drink every day?"

"No," he said, "Only when I don't have a job to do."

Robin thought no more of it. She handed him the plate of food. He thanked her for thinking of him. Fred was 6 feet 4, like a giant towering over Robin at 5 feet 3. He looked down at her and kissed her on the cheek.

"What was that for?" Robin asked innocently.

"For being so thoughtful, I get this urge when I'm near you," Fred replied.

"What kind of urge, Fred?"

"You know how a man gets when he's near a woman. Like butterflies in my stomach."

Robin just looked at him with a strange look on her face, wondering what Fred was trying to say.

"You make me nervous, sweet thing. What are you doing to me? Can I be with you, Robin? Can I hold you?"

Robin, not knowing how to react to Fred's forwardness, was nervous because he had caught her off guard. She didn't want to hurt his feelings or destroy the friendship. Robin knew she had to choose her words carefully.

"Fred, you're funny. I like you a lot. But we're not ready for what I think you're trying to say to me. Let's take it slow, OK?"

"If that's what you feel, Robin. It's been five years since I've been with a woman, and I got this burning in my soul for you. I think of you every minute. I hear love songs on the radio, and every one reminds me of you. I can't sleep at night, and when I do I dream of you. I sit waiting for hours for you to come by."

Robin was speechless. She didn't know what to say except "I'd better get going. It's late, and I have to work in the morning."

"Robin, wait. Can I just hold your hand, please?" Fred begged as if his life depended on it. He held her hand and walked her to the car. "Can I see you tomorrow? Please come."

"I'll be here after work, Fred. See you then." Robin took off, leaving dust behind her.

What am I going to do? She was thinking. *I like Fred, but I don't want to be intimate with him. He hasn't been with anyone in five years! He might kill me! I need to go talk to Ellen.*

She called Ellen. "Ellen, girl, wake up. I need to talk to you.

"Is everything OK, Robin? Your mom all right?"

29

"Yeah, girl. I need to talk to you. Fred came on to me today."

"Say what? It's 10 o'clock. You should be in bed."

"I know, but I had to talk to somebody. I might give in to him. Ellen, what should I do?"

"Girl, I can't tell you what to do. Follow your heart. We'll talk tomorrow at work."

Robin's phone was ringing.

"Girl, you up?" Robin could just barely hear Raine on the other end of the phone.

"Girl, what time is it?"

"It's almost 3:30. You better make moves or you'll be late."

"OK, Raine, thanks. I'm up."

Robin had hardly slept a wink all night. She kept thinking how long it had been since she'd been with a man. *Fred's not my type,* she kept telling herself, *but what is my type?* All night she had battled with her mind.

When she got to work, her friend Weesee said, "Robin, girlfriend, you look tired as hell."

Robin said, "What's going on Weesee?"

Weesee was off the meter. The girl was a trip. She was real about everything, and you'd have to know Weesee to relate to her. She was hilarious, always kept everyone at work laughing. She'd break real-life issues down to you in a way where you'd be like, "She ain't never lied, and that's so true." The girl was deep.

Weesee said, "Robin, girl, I know you ain't had no dick working these long 12 hours. If I had a man all he could do is look, 'cause I'm so damn tired I can fall down. So tell me something…"

Robin was laughing at her, because Weesee was so animated with different facial expressions you couldn't help but laugh. Robin said, "Weesee, girl, I couldn't sleep last night. I had some things on my mind."

Weesee said, "Things on your mind? Shoot, I got things on my damn mind too, like how the hell I can make me some more money; 12 hours just ain't gettin' it for me. I'll tell you what, Robin. If I had me a man, you better damn well believe I wouldn't be working these long hours."

"It's rough!" Robin agreed.

Weesee said, "See, if I were like you, living at home with my Mom, I'd have a little change in my pocket. But I got rent, gas and electric, phone, car note and every damn thing looking me in the face like it's my man. I say it like that, 'cause I got to take care of it. What the hell you got on your mind?"

Raine was on the floor laughing. Weesee had that kind of effect on people. Robin said, "Weesee, girl, I just need some sleep."

Weesee said, "You sure do, 'cause you look worn out, like you been working that thang all night. I tell you what, don't bring your ass in the ladies' room at break time, 'cause I got the chair, and I'm going to sit my tired black behind down. You should take your sleepy ass to sleep at night. I'll check you later, Robin."

"OK, Wees. Do you know where Ellen is working?"

"No, but I'm sure she's around here somewhere trying to save somebody's soul."

Robin said, "Wees, go take your nap. Girl, you too much!"

Robin had to talk to Ellen. "Ellen, girl," she said, "I had to call you last night. I hardly got any sleep, and I'm feeling it. I think I like Fred, and I don't know what to do."

Ellen said, "Robin, girl, I thought I was dreaming when you called. Did you say to me you were thinking about knocking boots with him?"

"You wasn't that sleepy," Robin said. "You got that part. Ellen, I don't know what to do. It worried me so last night. I came to the realization that I really like this man."

Ellen said, "Well that don't make you sleep with him. Why don't you get to know him better, see if it builds into something? Maybe date. Robin, I'm your best friend, and you've been through a lot since the death of your dad. Give yourself a chance. Love will find you, and you'll know it when it comes. Robin, you deserve the best."

"Ellen, you're right; maybe I'm reading too much into this. Maybe I'm just lonely and like the attention. You know my heart stopped at Gerald. Fred is nothing like Gerald, but it was cute the way he came on to me. Kinda sweet and innocent."

"Get to know him better," Ellen said, "That's all I got to say about it. Innocence can sometimes be scary, 'cause then you have to teach him. Kinda like a baby in the world knowing nothing about life. Do you want a child or a man? Just take your time."

"Ellen you're right. See, that's why I call on you. That why you're my best girl. Do you think I should avoid him, maybe stay away?" Robin asked.

"Follow your heart, Robin. If he makes you laugh and you enjoy him, then capture every minute."

"Thanks, Ellen, just for being you."

Just then Weesee butted in. "Robin, girl, we only got four hours to go. My damn feet hurt, and I'm ready to get the hell up and out of here. These hours are kickin' my ass, but the money keeps me hanging. Girl, I got to hit a lottery or something."

Robin said, "Wees, I'm feeling it, too. Straight to bed for me when I get home."

Raine said, "I'll see you tomorrow night, girl. Only two more to go. At least we get to sleep in in the morning. I'll see you tomorrow, Robin. Get some sleep."

Robin said, "OK, Raine, you get some rest, too."

Everybody was racing out to the parking lot, headed in different directions. Robin let out a sigh of relief after her long work day. Her

I NEVER MEANT TO MAKE YOU CRY

body was telling her to go home and relax, but she had Fred on her mind. She drove by the apartment, and there he was, waiting outside.

Fred said, "Hi, Robin, you came. Listen; about yesterday…I didn't want to frighten you off. I only wanted to tell you how I was feeling. Get out the car; stay with me a while. I promise I won't bite."

Robin said, "Fred, I really can't stay long. I'm exhausted. I just wanted to check and make sure you were OK."

Fred said, "I'm fine now that I've seen you. Why don't you come inside for a while? Maybe get something to eat. Let me cook for you."

"No thanks, Fred. I really need to get moving. Maybe I'll stop back over after my night shift is over on my way home."

"That will be nice. I'll make breakfast for you," Fred said.

"I'll see you later, Fred," Robin said.

She was thinking, *Why did I tell him I'd be there early in the morning after work, when I know I should go home and get some sleep after working all night?* Deep down she knew she wanted to be with him.

When she walked into the house, Robin said, "Ma, how you feeling today? How was your day?" She was glad her mom kept busy with church activities. That kept her mind occupied, and it was good for her to be around people. Her mom and dad had been dedicated to each other. Having been married for 35 years, all they had were each other. After Dad died, Mom had to make a new life for herself. Robin had always admired the commitment in her parent's relationship. They had believed in till death did them part, and that was the way it was. Robin longed for that solid commitment, but how could she have that unless she allowed herself a chance to be involved with someone? Robin was feeling as if now that she was getting older she was ready to settle down, build a foundation, and have a solid relationship. *I've got to give myself a chance*, she thought.

On the night shift, Robin asked, "Weesee, you ready to do this long night? I got plenty of sleep."

Weesee said, "I can tell, girl. Your ass ain't dragging like yesterday. I just want to get this over 'cause my lottery number came out last night and my pocket is empty.

Robin said, "Good for you, Weesee. Maybe one day you'll hit big enough to leave this place for good.

Weesee said, "I hope the hell you're right, 'cause I'm ready to be out; it's been too long."

When the night shift was over, the parking lot was like the racetrack, everybody racing to get home.

Robin went by Fred's. It was 5:30 in the morning, still dark out. Again she hated that he didn't have a phone. She rang the bell, and Fred came to the door.

Robin said, "Good morning, Fred."

Fred said, "Good morning, Robin. Come in. I made you breakfast, and I've got the coffee going. I'm all ready for you."

Robin walked inside. Fred had the little table out. The aroma was kickin'. The kitchen was too small for two people to be in. It would have been a tight fit. Robin was impressed, and she loved the attention. She was so exhausted from the long night. She didn't want to hurt Fred's feelings by not eating.

Fred said, "Sit down, Robin. Make yourself comfortable." He went into the kitchen to prepare the food. Robin turned on the TV to

37

catch the early news. Breakfast was nothing fancy, but Robin could tell Fred had put his heart into it. After they finished eating, they watched TV. Fred was very quiet and just sat staring at Robin.

Finally he said, "Robin, did you enjoy your breakfast?"

Robin said, "Yes, it was delicious. Thank you so much. That was nice of you."

"When you care about someone," Fred said, "You do special things."

He got up from the table and came to sit on the small sofa where Robin was sitting. He pushed her back and kissed her. They both got caught up in the moment. Robin didn't resist the kiss. When the kiss ended, Fred was panting like a dog. He took a deep breath and apologized.

"I'm sorry. I just wanted to know what you taste like. I'm never like this with any woman. Please forgive me. I feel butterflies in my stomach."

Robin was shaking. Fred's aggressiveness had caught her by surprise, but she liked it. She liked the feeling it gave her. She hadn't kissed anyone in a long time. Different sensations were going through her body. She wanted more. Before she knew it she blurted out: "Fred, make love to me!"

She stopped and shook her head. "I'm sorry I said that. I must leave. I just got caught up in this kiss, and it's late, it's too early...I don't know what I'm saying. I need to get home."

Fred grabbed her hand. "I want you, Robin," he said, "Let me have you!"

She sent him to the store for condoms. Shaking in her clothes, she was nervous, but not too nervous to remember that they had to practice safe sex. She was thinking, *Is this the right thing to do? Maybe I'll feel different when he comes back.*

Fred must have run to the store, because it seemed all of five minutes before he was back. He seemed just as nervous as she was. His face was sweating. Robin didn't know if it was because he had run to the store or if it was the anticipation of making love. He drew the drapes in the small room, came closer with trembling hands, kissed her and, before she knew it, they were in the heat of passion.

The aftershock of what had just taken place was obvious to both of them. Her hair was wild and all over the place. Her body was drenched with sweat. The sweat of the body heat between the two of them was heavy. The old couch bed was so small there was no air between them.

Immediately she made her way to the bathroom to clean herself up. Reality slapped her in the face and she thought *what did I just do?* Although the sex had given her good feelings, when it was over she felt it was all wrong. She stayed locked in the bathroom for what felt like an eternity, feeling embarrassed and ashamed, because she had had selfish motives. The only reason she had given in to temptation was to be satisfied sexually. She had been unable to resist.

How could she face Fred now? What could she say? Could she act as if nothing had happened between them? How was he going to react to her? What now? Robin's head was full of unresolved questions without answers, without reason for her selfishness. What was she going to do with Fred? She had to get her composure intact.

She opened the door slowly. Fred was lying on the tiny couch bed staring straight at the ceiling, eyes fixed, with a wide grin on his face. Robin's first reaction was, *Is he dead?* He was stiff as a corpse with a death look, but a happy death look. Robin called his name.

I NEVER MEANT TO MAKE YOU CRY

"Fred! Fred! Are you OK? Are you all right?"

There was no answer at first. She just knew she had killed him. He was dead. She panicked; her palms were beginning to sweat. *What am I going to do? Should I leave him? Do I call Ellen? Wake up, Fred, say something!*

Fred smiled at her. The first words he said were, "Babe, Robin, you're the best! I feel like I died and came back again. I'm a new man, all because of you."

Robin said, "Fred, we need to talk. This shouldn't have happened."

Fred said, "Robin, do you know how long it's been for me? I feel so good right now I can rebuild every house on this street. Girl, you give me energy; you take my breath away. You put a smile on my face. I've never felt like this before. Never, ever. Please stay with me. Make me brand-new again."

Robin said, "Fred, I've got to go. I'm sorry!"

She ran out of the apartment, leaving Fred in what sounded like heaven for him. Robin was torn with emotions, overly exhausted from work the night before and the work Fred had just performed on her.

She went straight to Ellen's house. Blinded with emotions, she was frantic. *How and why did I allow this to happen?* Robin tortured herself all the way to Ellen's. She began banging on the door.

"Ellen, wake up, wake up!"

It was 11 a.m., and Ellen was knocked out from a long night of work. She dragged to the door, and slowly opened it. She saw Robin and said, "What's wrong? Is it your mom? What's so urgent?"

Robin said, "I'm so sorry to wake you, but I just made love to Fred. Girl, get some coffee in you. Wake up, talk to me. What am I going to do now?"

Ellen's eyes popped wide open like she'd drank a whole pot of coffee. Her eyes got wider than golf balls. She said, "Girl, you did it. What happened, when and where?"

Robin said, "I should have gone home right after work, but I stopped by Fred's. He cooked breakfast and one thing led to another, and it just happened."

Ellen said, "I hope you used some form of protection."

Robin looked insulted. "Give me some credit, of course I did. Ellen, I was thinking solely of myself, getting my kicks off. I just got caught up in the passion, and I found myself helpless wanting this man. Since Gerald, there's been no one, and when he kissed me, all kinds of signals and alarms woke my body up. I was asleep, and then I awakened to a sexual encounter and not love. Ellen, I left the apartment speechless, unable to face him or myself."

"Robin, stop torturing yourself," Ellen said. "You're human. You're not made of stone. Look, it's a done deal now. Don't beat yourself up, especially if you enjoyed the feeling it gave you. Look at all the stress you've been under. Your dad's death, caring for your mom, and work. Don't you deserve to let yourself go?"

Robin said, "Ellen, I lost myself in the moment. I don't love him; he's not my type of guy. Don't get me wrong, he makes me laugh, and he's attentive in his own way, but there's a lot missing. He doesn't give me that feeling Gerald gave me. How could I give myself to him when I can't feel like that for him? He doesn't even have a job."

"Girl, relax, OK? Of course he'll never measure up to Gerald. No other man in this lifetime will. You're going to meet others and fall for them, but believe me, every love will be different. One day you'll even find someone to love greater than Gerald. The man you've waited for, for so long. Live for today. What just happened is past now. Get a hold of yourself and keep moving. Enjoy Fred for Fred," Ellen said.

"Ellen, you're right," Robin agreed. "Thank you, girl, for being my sounding board and a good friend. What would I do without you?" She got up to leave. "I'd better let you get back to sleep. We've got one more night to do. We'll talk at work. Oh, and remember, Ellen -- please don't say anything to anyone."

"I promise," Ellen said. "See you tonight, girl."

"Love you and thanks," Robin said.

The drive home seemed endless. Robin's mind was a blur. She was mentally and emotionally exhausted. As she pulled into the driveway, she parked the car, put her head on the steering wheel and cried. Warm tears streamed down her face because she was beat.

Beat from the pressures of a lifetime trying to pick up where her dad had left off, working a long 12-hour shift and keeping her family together. She was on overload. Where did she have room for someone else or even her own pleasures? She laid her head down on the steering wheel and slept.

At work, Weesee said, "Robin, girl, what's up with the scarf on your head? Now, you just got a new hair-do last week. I know it's the night shift and all, but see, you can't fool me. That's the kind of scarf you'd wear soon after you been laying up sweating with a man and your hair-do just gone to the dogs. Don't think you can fool me. I know what I'm talking about. Did the nigga have any money? That's all I got to say."

Robin said, "Weesee, it nothing like that at all. I just slept late and didn't have time to do my hair."

Weesee said, "Girl, you need to stop frontin' with me. Been there, done that. All I got to say is, make sure the nigga has got some loot and you got paid. See, there's a lot of dirty dicks out there wanting something for nothing. You make sure you get yours, 'cause

I damn sure is gonna get mine. The nigga better have Rent, Gas and Electric money, phone bill or something or he don't get any honey. Got it? No money, no honey!"

"Got it, Weesee," Robin said.

Weesee said, "See, maybe you don't need no money, but Weesee need plenty of money, honey, 'cause Weesee got bills to pay, and a man can't speak my name let alone get between these legs without the Benjamin's. Bring it to Weesee, Daddy. I'll call out his name all night as long as he's paying. Without the money, honey, Weesee get funny. "That's why I got to do these long-ass hours. If I had a man, a rich one at that, I'll be damned if you see me here all night long. Hell, I'm ready to sleep right now and we've got five hours to go. It's a trip."

Robin said, "I know, Weesee, it's long. I got plenty of sleep today. Slept like a baby."

"I bet you did." Weesee's eyebrows were raised, suspicious about the way Robin had been acting lately.

Robin said, "What's going on Raine? You having a good night? We're busy; that helps. How are the boys doing?"

Raine said, "They're doing good. School will be starting soon. I need to make some overtime to get their school clothes."

Robin said, "I hear you, girl; knock yourself out. Do what you gotta do. I've got enough on my plate. I'm so tired these days I can't work it."

With another long work day completed, Robin looked for Ellen. She had been a no-show for work. Robin, feeling guilty, thought that it was because she woke Ellen out of a sound sleep and maybe she had overslept.

Robin said, "Raine, I'll see you later. Have a nice weekend." Robin reached for her cell phone to call Ellen to make sure she was OK.

Ellen picked up on the second ring. "Hello?"

Robin said, "Hey, girl, what happened to you? You didn't make it to work."

"I overslept," Ellen sighed. "I got dressed and was going to come in late, and then the car gave out on me."

"Ellen, I'm sorry," Robin said apologetically. "I shouldn't have come over disturbing you. Why didn't you call for a ride?"

"Robin, really, it's no big deal; that's what friends are for," Ellen said with a smile. "I'm just tired, girl. I needed the night off. When I decided to come in and do six hours, the car was dead. I couldn't see calling you at work."

Robin said, "Listen, do you need to go anywhere? I'm just going home to sleep. You can use my car if you need it. I can stop by on my way home. I'll stop by Fred's to see if he can fix your car. I'm sure he won't charge me much. That's what friends are for. Plus that gives me an excuse to see how he reacts after our encounter together."

Ellen said, "Robin, that's a good idea. I don't need to go anywhere right now. I'm all set. Call me when you get home, Robin. Just enjoy the moment."

Robin rang the bell to Fred's apartment. It was 6:00 in the morning. Fred wouldn't be sitting out this time of the morning waiting for her. It was still dark out. Fred came to the door. He said something, but his speech was slurred, and Robin couldn't understand him.

"Good morning, Fred. Don't I at least get a 'hello'?" Robin could smell the stench of alcohol on his breath. She was trying to decide if she should stay out or go inside.

"Robin, come in out of the rain. I was just about to make coffee."

"Have you been drinking, Fred?" Robin asked emphatically. "Do you have a drinking problem? Maybe I should come back some other time."

Fred grabbed her arm, pushed her against the wall and said to her, "You're not leaving me now. I stayed up all night waiting for you. You come inside, Robin."

Robin jerked her arm away, shocked by his actions. She knew he was drunk now, because of his temperament. "Let me go, Fred! You're hurting me. Let me go!!"

Robin ran to her car. Fred, following her, picked up a two-by-four and shot it through the windshield of her car. He was screaming at her. "You walked into my life and now you want out? I'm not going to let you go. Stay with me, Robin! Come back!"

All the drama awakened the neighbors. Someone called the police. The windshield was shattered and so was Robin.

What had she done? Fred was a madman, out of control, under the influence of alcohol. All she wanted to do was ask him about fixing Ellen's car. Someone had called the police. Robin was a nervous wreck. And to think she had slept with this man. The police asked Robin if she wanted to press charges for the broken windshield. She said no. She was hysterical; she just wanted to leave. She got into her car and drove off as fast as she could.

Robin went straight to Ellen's house, the wind and rain blowing through her windshield. *How am I going to explain this? Ellen is the only person I can tell. What was wrong with Fred? Why did he react like a crazy person?* Robin didn't want to upset her mom. She didn't want her mom to think she'd been in an accident, so she made up her mind to stay over at Ellen's and get the windshield fixed as soon as possible.

Ellen came to the door. Robin was shaking like a leaf, frightened, nervous and shook up by what had just happened.

Robin said, "Ellen, he was like a crazy drunk person. He didn't want me to leave and he threw a piece of wood through my windshield to stop me from going. He scared me to death. Please, I can't go home like this; my mom will worry herself sick. It all happened so fast, without warning."

"Robin, you can't go back there. Stay away from him. What made him react like that?" Ellen asked worriedly.

"I think he'd been drinking, and my sleeping with him has made him obsessive. I'm afraid. Please don't tell anyone," Robin pleaded. "I have to fix the windshield right away. First I should call my mom to tell her I'm staying over with you for the night and I'll be home tomorrow."

Ellen said, "Good idea; call your mom while I get you something to relax you. Girl, you are a wreck."

Robin called her mother. "Mom, listen I'm over at Ellen's. We're working on a project. I'm going to stay overnight here. Call me if you need anything."

Her mom said, "Robin, are you OK? You don't sound too good. Where's Ellen? Is everything all right over there?"

"Mom, I'm fine, just tired from a long night. Ellen and I are going to go car shopping, and I'm just going to stay over and hang out with the girls. Do you mind?" Robin tried to calm her.

Her mom said, "Robin dear, you're young, you should have fun, but you sound…"

Robin cut in on her mom and assured her that she was fine and to call her if she needed anything.

"Is your mom OK? She knew something was wrong, didn't she?" Ellen asked.

"Ellen, I had to lie. My mom knows me. I just don't want her to worry," Robin confessed.

"Why don't you take a long shower, lie down and rest your nerves, and we'll talk when you're rested. You've been up all night and you just had a traumatic experience. If your mom calls, I'll cover for you," Ellen comforted her.

"My head is pounding. I need to lie down. Thanks for being my friend. I'm going upstairs. We'll talk later."

Robin tossed and turned in bed, wondering what she had done to bring the rage out in Fred. She knew that she had to stay away from him because he could fly off the handle at any moment. With her head pounding and eyes red from crying, she finally fell off to sleep. It was late in the evening when the phone rang; it was Robin's mom.

Ellen answered the phone. "Hello?"

Robin's mom said, "Hi, Ellen, this is Mrs. Jacobs. Is Robin there?"

"Hi, Mrs. Jacobs, how are you doing? Robin went to lie down for a nap. If it's important, I can wake her."

"No, baby, let her rest; just give her a message for me please. Tell her a young man named Fred has called several times looking for her."

"I'll give her the message, Mrs. Jacobs. Are you OK? Are you home alone?" Ellen asked.

Mrs. Jacobs said, "I'm fine, Ellen, and the grandkids are with me. You girls have fun and good luck car shopping."

"Thank you, Mrs. Jacobs. I'll give Robin the message as soon as she wakes up. Take care. Talk to you soon."

Robin was all worn out, and her anxiety showed in her face as she made her way into the kitchen, where Ellen was preparing dinner.

Ellen asked, "How did you sleep, Robin? You've been out for hours. Your mom called earlier to say you had several phone calls from Fred."

"Oh, no! What if he said something to my mom? Why is he calling me? What could he say or want with me?" Robin worried.

"Calm down, Robin. Your mom sounded fine, no different than she normally does. Stop panicking. We have to think about getting your windshield replaced. I called several places while you were asleep to get estimates. In the morning we'll get it fixed like new."

"I don't know what I'd do without you, Ellen. Was my mom OK? Were the kids with her?"

"She's fine, and yes the kids are there so she's not alone. I want you to get a grip, get yourself together. Don't worry; together we'll get through this, but you need to stay away from Fred until things die down."

"I promise, Ellen. I won't go over there again. I'm afraid to."

Robin and Ellen had a nice quiet evening watching movies. The next morning they got Robin's car fixed like new.

The weekend was over, and it was back to the long work week. Robin was having a problem staying focused. She kept thinking about what had taken place with Fred. Somehow she knew that wouldn't be the end of him. She had never dealt with anyone who had a drinking problem. She wondered if he realized how out of control he was, how different he was when he was drinking.

All day she isolated herself from Raine and Weesee. She kept a low profile. Her excuse was that she wasn't feeling very well. Ellen knew differently. Ellen was worried about her friend staying away from Fred for good.

After work, everyone raced for the parking lot. Robin found her car and noticed several notes sticking out of the door. They were from Fred. She said good-bye to everyone. Waiting for Ellen to come out so she could give her a ride home, Robin opened and read the notes. The first one read, "Robin, I'm sorry. Please let me reimburse you for the damages done." She opened the second note, which read, "I never meant to hurt you. Please forgive me, Fred."

Robin took both notes and crumbled them in her hand. Ellen was on her way to the car. Robin didn't tell her about the notes; she kept them to herself. Robin took Ellen home first, and then she went home herself. Robin just wanted a quiet evening to herself. She wanted to erase Fred from her memory. She was home relaxing in her bedroom when the doorbell rang.

Her mom called up the stairs. "Robin, the young man who fixed the flooded basement is here. I believe his name is Ed. Will you come down?"

Robin's hands began to sweat. She couldn't yell down to tell her mom to send him away; her mom would get suspicious. She got dressed, took her time and strolled down the stairs. There was Fred standing in the foyer.

Fred said, "Hi, Robin. Please let me talk to you. I left several notes on your car."

Before Fred could get another word out, Robin interrupted him by saying, "Let's go outside and talk." Once outside, she said, "Fred, you had no right to come here. What do you want from me? What's wrong with you? I don't want my mom knowing about what's happened. She's been through enough."

Fred said, "Robin, I'm sorry; it won't happen again. I had one too many beers. I lost control of myself. Please forgive me. I'll never do anything to hurt you again. Please let me fix this. Give me a second chance."

Robin said, "Fred, second chances rarely come; they are few and far between."

Still, Robin gave in to him. A few years later they were married. Yes, it was the Cinderella wedding, the one she had dreamed of from the time she was a child, but all to the wrong man. Robin learned that second chances can be a very costly. After the wedding vows were exchanged, the truth about Fred came out. Not only did she not know about the drinking binges, but she later learned about his drug addiction. Fred was arrested three years into the marriage and sent to federal prison for selling drugs. Robin saw that as her way out and didn't look back. She divorced Fred, and tried to put the memories and pain behind her. She had a new lease on life.

Be careful who you give your heart to, she thought. Robin realized after years of recovery that she had tried to hide her grief, pretending to love someone when all she did was compromise love to hide hurt. She had never allowed herself time to cry or feel pain when she lost her dad. She hid her sorrows and tears in the laughter that Fred gave her, only to feel those tears later in their marriage.

Westchester, 3 years later

Robin moved on with life, surrounding herself with family and friends. She even built up the strength to let go of her mom. She knew that her dad's shoes could never be filled, and that her mom had to find life all over again for herself.

During the hardship of her marriage to Fred with all its abuse and pain, Robin lost Sydney to lung cancer. She lost her best friend, but she was so grateful to Sydney for rearing their son on the right path. Larry was now in college, in his sophomore year, and Robin was gaining the years back that she had wasted on Fred. She was happy about her mom's independence. Everyone had their own agenda and was moving on with life.

Robin continued to work long hours. Living at home alone with Larry away was at times lonely, but when she looked back on all the drama with Fred, she appreciated the peace. Robin spent a lot of time with her girlfriend Ellen taking nice vacations. They both felt they worked hard enough to enjoy some of the finer things in life. She kept in touch with Raine, who relocated to Atlanta and never lost contact with Weesee.

Weesee got lucky, met a suave dude with money, and now lived in Virginia. Robin had friends who were dear and close. Once a week, she babysat for her nieces. She hadn't been in the dating world for four years. After the divorce, she focused on herself. She was afraid to put her heart on her sleeve. She kept to herself until she met Oscar O'Neil.

Robin remembered March 12th as if it were yesterday. That was the day Oscar James O'Neil, otherwise known as O.J., walked into her life. Winters were very cold in Westchester, New York. Larry, while he was at home for spring break, kept reminding his mother to get the furnace cleaned. Robin was so preoccupied with work and classes she had forgotten about Larry's suggestion. March 12th was a cold, cold winter night, and the furnace died suddenly.

Robin felt that she was a marked target for things dying out on her. She had no other option but to call an emergency heating company. She searched the Yellow Pages to see who serviced 24 hours. It was 10 p.m. There was no way she could sleep in the house; it was like a refrigerator. She phoned S.O.S Heating Service, which advertised itself as the "on the spot heating company." They told her someone would be out as soon as possible.

Thirty minutes later, Oscar O'Neil was at her door. He was pecan brown, medium height, with a muscular build, clean-cut hair, a thick black mustache, white pearly teeth, and the most beautiful dark brown eyes she'd ever seen. Robin was immediately attracted to him. No one had captured her attention in this way in years. He was very polite in speaking, with a strong, solid voice. He introduced himself as Oscar O'Neil and gave her his personal business card.

She then escorted him to the basement where the problem was. He assured her that he'd do all he could to get her heat working properly, quickly and efficiently. He began to make conversation about the weather and how cold it was that night. Robin had a portable heater running in the kitchen, the only part of the house that was warm.

As he worked in the basement, O.J. explained to Robin that he couldn't get used to the cold weather. He told her he was from Florida and would be returning home within the next three weeks. He told her that he was on the job training and working towards his degree. Robin was impressed knowing he was a long way from home.

"Mr. O'Neil, please forgive my manners. Can I offer you something to drink?" Robin asked.

"No, thank you," O.J. said. "Please call me O.J.; everyone does."

"O.J., since you're not used to our cold weather, how did you end up coming to Westchester?" Robin queried.

"Ms. Jacobs, I'm working on my degree, and S.O.S. Company offered an eight-week course with the credits I needed to finish."

"Please call me Robin. So you've been here for five weeks? Have you done much? I mean seen much of our little city?"

"As a matter of fact, I haven't to either question. I keep very long hours; by the time my days end it's too late to do anything. I don't really know anyone here in Westchester."

"Where are you staying?" Robin asked.

"I'm downtown at the Holiday Inn. In fact, all the guys who are from out of town taking the course are staying on the same floor of the hotel."

"So you've met a lot of new associates?" Robin asked.

"Not really; everyone has a different schedule. I never see my roommate. Only three weeks left, and then I'm home," O.J. replied politely.

"It'll be nice to get home to some warm weather. I imagine you have a wife waiting?" Robin asked inquisitively.

"I'm not married, never been married. Maybe one day," O.J. answered.

"I'm sorry. I didn't mean to be nosy."

"It's not a big deal. Are you married?" O.J. inquired.

"Actually, I'm divorced," Robin said.

They both made eye contact.

"Looks like the furnace is up and running again. If you turn the thermostat all the way up, Robin, I can hear it kick in and you'll be back to normal."

O.J. checked Robin out as she went up the stairs. He knew that the attraction was too strong to leave there without a phone number. Meanwhile Robin was thinking, *How can I see this man again?* There was something about him that piqued her curiosity. She didn't want to be aggressive and scare him off, but she knew she wanted to see him again.

O.J. yelled from the basement. "It just kicked over. She's up and running again."

As he headed up the stairs, Robin greeted him with gratefulness, "Thank you so much, O.J. How much do I owe you?"

"I'll tell you what. If you'll have dinner with me and show me some of Westchester, we can call it even."

Robin hesitated to accept the offer. But knowing she wanted to see this man again, she said, "It's a deal. But with only one condition -- you have something to drink with me right now. "

"It's a deal, then. Coffee would be nice," O.J. smiled.

"Coffee it is, then. How do you take it?" Robin asked.

"Black and sweet, like I like my women. The sweeter the better."

Robin flirted with him, "Black and sweet, huh?"

With a huge smile on her face, she made the coffee. They were out in the kitchen talking for hours. Both were amazed at how much they had in common. They both loved horror movies and most of the same foods. Robin felt very comfortable in O.J.'s presence.

O.J. looked at his watch. "I think I've overstayed my welcome. I'd better get moving. About that dinner...I have your phone number from when you called the company. I'll call you tomorrow after I look at my schedule. Is that OK with you?"

Robin said, "That's fine, O.J. I work long hours so if I'm not at home leave me a number to reach you."

On the back of his business card, O.J. wrote the phone number to his personal cell phone, the hotel number and his pager number. He made sure he covered all bases. He definitely wanted to see her again. Robin, thanking him again, walked him to the door.

"I enjoyed our talk, Robin."

"So did I."

"I'll give you a call tomorrow."

"That sounds good. Take care. Good night," Robin said as she waved good-bye.

"Good night, Robin. Stay warm and lock up. Call me if there are any problems."

Robin liked the idea that he was protective. She listened while he stood behind the door until she put the locks on. She watched him as he brushed the snow off the van. He sat in the driveway until the van heated up, then he drove off. Robin watched until the van was out of sight.

Robin completed another long workday. Things were different at work with Raine and Weesee gone, and Ellen had gotten promoted and moved to another building. Robin was taking business classes to complete her degree, which would open doors for a career change. And since she didn't have class tonight, she thought she'd phone Ellen to see what her plans were. Robin didn't feel like being alone.

Ellen answered on the second ring. "Hello?"

"Hey, girl, how you doing?"

"I'm OK. Looking in this empty fridge of mine for dinner," Ellen said.

"Perfect timing. Why don't we meet for Chinese? I've got something to share with you."

"Sounds good; give me an hour and I'll meet you at our favorite spot."

"Perfect. Later."

At the Restaurant with Ellen

Robin arrived first. She waited for Ellen to show. Ellen had always been a procrastinator and was never on time for anything. O.J. ran across Robin's mind; she wondered if he'd called. She hadn't been home yet to check her messages; maybe good news awaited her. Ellen arrived.

"It's about time you made it! I'm starving!" Robin teased her.

"Well, let's go get our grub on; I'm ready."

They sat at their table. They both ordered the all-you-can-eat buffet. "Ellen, how's the new job coming?" Robin asked.

"It's challenging, and the hours are just as long, but I'm using my brain now. I like the people; everyone is so nice."

"Ellen, you've always been a people person, and you're very good at what you do. I imagine sales will go up with your marketing skills. So have you met any attractive men?"

"Nope, I haven't met anyone yet, and work is all that I'm good at. I can't seem to find the right man. All the good ones are either married or dead. So I give up. Besides, with my new position I have enough on my plate. Not to change the subject, but have you heard from Raine or Weesee?"

"Weesee called last week. She left a message on the machine saying she was in Aruba with someone tall black and handsome and he had plenty of money. All she could say was 'Lordy lordy, Lord, I hit the jackpot!' I laughed when I heard that. So she's fine. I spoke with Raine a few days ago; she and the boys are good. They both said to tell you hello."

"How's Larry adjusting to college?" Ellen asked.

"He's doing good. I miss him so much. You know he thinks he's my man. He calls every chance he gets to check on me. I told him to call on the weekends and not to worry about me. I have enough to keep me occupied. Plus the phone bill is outrageous. He's fine, and said he received your package. That was nice of you to send him a gift box."

"Well, he is my godson. I just want him to have all he needs," Ellen said.

"Thanks. Listen, Ellen, the thing I wanted to tell you is, I met a guy. He's so cute."

Ellen looked surprised. "Do tell. When and where?"

"Last night he came out to service my furnace. When I first laid eyes on him, the attraction was there. We talked for hours. He's supposed to call for a dinner date."

Ellen said, "Girl, that's good. You haven't smiled like that in years. Is he available?"

"I suppose so. He said he wasn't married, but he lives in Florida."

"Florida?" Ellen questioned. "What is he doing here in Westchester fixing your furnace?"

Robin said, "He's been here for several weeks on a work-study program for the company he works for, which will enable him to complete his degree. He's only here for three more weeks."

"Sounds like he's got it going on. Where is he staying?" Ellen asked with a wink.

"Downtown, at the Holiday Inn. Ellen, he's got the darkest bedroom eyes I've ever seen, almost piercing. And he's a good conversationalist. We hit it off good."

"So, when are you guys going to dinner?"

"Soon, I hope," Robin responded. "He's got to get back to me on his schedule. I'm looking forward to seeing him again."

"Are you nervous, Robin? I know how hard it is for you to trust anyone after Fred."

"I am, but it's only a dinner date. I'm not looking for anything serious," Robin said matter of factly.

Ellen said, "Girl, you never know what could happen. I'm just glad you're giving yourself a chance again. Wear something sexy."

"It'll be nice to be in the company of an intelligent man who's on the rise. He says he wants to start his own business once he completes his degree."

"Interesting. Maybe he'll settle down here in Westchester!" Ellen said.

"You never know." They both laughed!

Robin and Ellen finished their dinner and said their good-byes. Robin went home to a warm house. She's walked in, threw her bag on the bed and went straight for her answering machine. The answering machine was blinking. She had two messages.

First she heard Larry's voice. "Hi, Mom. I know it's not the weekend. Just called to say I aced my chemistry test and to tell you I love you. Holla at you soon."

The second voice was O.J.'s. "Hello, Robin. Thought we could get together on Saturday if your schedule isn't full. Please call me on my cell number at any time day or night to let me know if Saturday is good for you. Hope to hear from you soon."

Robin was smiling from ear to ear. She didn't want to seem too anxious. She figured she'd stall him for a day, and then return the call. She was both nervous and excited to hear from him.

O.J. couldn't wait. He called her.

Robin picked up the phone. "Hello?"

O.J. said, "Hi, how are you doing?"

"I'm fine O.J. Hey, about Saturday, that's a good time for me."

"I'll pick you up around 7 p.m. if that's OK with you," O.J. said.

"Seven will be fine," Robin confirmed.

Robin's hands were trembling at the sound of his masculine voice on the other end of the receiver. She felt like a high school girl going out on her very first date. She felt anxious and excited. She thought it was time to go shopping for a new outfit, and decided to bring Ellen along for her opinion. Robin felt that a whole new makeover would do her good, plus she hadn't pampered herself in years.

Robin and Ellen made a day of it. They started with an early breakfast. After breakfast they went to the spa, had a facial, nails and hair done. After the beauty makeover, they were ready to bargain hunt for sales.

Robin held up an outfit on a hanger. "Ellen, what do you think of this black pantsuit?"

"You go, sexy momma; that will knock him dead," Ellen encouraged her.

Robin was a full-figured woman with a tiny waistline, an hourglass shape with the curves in just the right areas. Almost anything she wore stood out.

"Ellen, you don't think this is too much, do you?"

"No. Robin, it's elegant, conservative and sexy. Believe me; your guy will take notice."

"OK, then this it is. I just have to get the accessories, and I'm all ready for Mr. O'Neil."

At O.J.'s hotel

O.J. was just as excited about their date. He knew from the moment he laid eyes on Robin that he had to see her again. At that moment he had forgotten that he had a woman and two kids in Florida with whom he shared his life. Although he'd been with this woman for over 20 years and she was the mother of his children, he couldn't bring himself to marry her. He'd been so preoccupied with raising his kids that marriage had never been an issue. O.J. vowed that because his father had run off and left his mom to raise him and his siblings alone, he would never do his kids that way.

He knew he stayed with this woman because of the kids. His relationship to her was an obligation. He provided for her and the kids by working two jobs, which meant there was never time for romance. He often wondered if he still loved this woman and how they had grown apart. The relationship was more like a business. He believed whatever it took to give his kids a healthy, stable life with a mom and dad was what mattered to him.

Robin was the first woman who'd captured his attention in a romantic sense. All O.J. had in mind up until he met Robin was finishing school and starting his business. Robin was very attractive and easy to talk with. Communication was the biggest problem he had with the woman he lived with. They worked opposite shifts, hadn't done things together as a couple for years. Their conversation was always about the kids or finances.

O.J. felt as if they were roommates. He was tired of pretending, putting on airs for other people to think they were the happiest couple alive. He buried himself in his career. He never gave any other woman a chance to know him. He was too busy. Robin was the first woman outside of his relationship that he ever paid any attention to.

He had a secret and didn't want to tell Robin of his relationship at home. He didn't want to risk knowing her, even in friendship, but O.J. couldn't let this opportunity pass. He'd never felt like this before. He didn't like the idea of not saying anything about his life in

Florida, but he only had three weeks left in Westchester. He wanted to know this woman.

O.J. felt that a little time was better than no time. Besides, how far could this go? He thought about what his brother used to say to him "All work and no play make O.J. a dull boy." He thought, *My brother is right. All these years I've worked my fingers to the bone to make a life for my children; now it's my time. Time for me to enjoy the finer things in life.* He thought Robin was the finest thing he'd ever laid eyes on. *It's time for me to be happy. Let me call my brother for encouragement.*

O.J. and his brother Aaron, whom everyone called A.J., were identical twins. As kids growing up they were very close and looked so much alike no one could tell them apart. O.J. was the elder by 15 minutes, but he always looked to A.J for advice when it came to women. As kids growing up with no dad and one sister, they had made a pact to always protect one another.

A.J. was smooth with the ladies, always juggled two, sometimes three women at a time. He lived a very flamboyant lifestyle, always traveling on the go making money. A.J. was a hustler and loved his women.

When he and O.J. were growing up, whenever one of them had a problem they'd always meet on the rooftop of the tall building in Brooklyn where they were raised, look out over the city and together figure out what to do. They'd call it their peace ground. As adults, they kept their peace ground meetings a tradition. O.J. thought, *I can't go to A.J. so I'll call him.*

"Hello?"

"What's up, man? How's thing going?" O.J. asked.

"I'm straight, man. What's up with you?" A.J. answered.

O.J. said, "Man, I'm still in Westchester trying to finish this class. It's cold as hell here."

"Man, you keep that cold weather; I'm under the AC as we speak. I went by to check on the home front for you. Everything is straight," A.J. said.

"Thanks, man," O.J. said. "I can always depend on my little brother to hold it down. Listen, I met someone, a woman."

A.J. was surprised. "You say what? You, Mr. Too Busy to Have a Life?"

O.J. laughed. "All right, all right, yes, me. Man, she's beautiful. I made a date with her for tomorrow night. A.J., man, I'm scared. I never told her I had someone at home."

"Man, is she beautiful? If you diggin' her, why does she need to know who you're with? Man, you're too straight for me. Didn't I teach you anything?" A.J. chided him.

"Hey, I like to be honest, and this secret is killing me, A.J., but if I tell her, I won't get a chance to be her man. I just know that about her. I feel it."

"O.J., listen up. You're only going to be there a short time. Enjoy the moment. Isn't that what I always tell you? Live for the moment. Stop sweatin' yourself about this honesty stuff. Enjoy yourself. Live for once. It's not like you're taking her to the altar. It's only a date. Besides me and you knowing, what are the chances of her finding out the truth with the distance?"

O.J. thought about it. "You're right."

"All right, then, get yourself together and do this. You are my twin, so don't be half-steppin' either. Show this woman what you're made of and have a good time," A.J. said.

"Thanks, man. Love you."

"Love you too. Bro. Later."

O.J. knew that A.J. would give him the confidence he lacked. They were identical in looks, but their personalities were like night and day. A.J. had always been the brave one, the twin who took risks at any cost. A.J. wasn't the type to settle down with one woman. He'd always say "Why settle for one when you have a variety to chose from?" That was his lifestyle: women and money. O.J. was the opposite. He believed in family, settling down and being more laid back and reserved.

O.J. wanted this date to be a memorable date. He wanted memories he could take back to Florida with him, memories he could reflect on when loneliness set in. He was starving for affection, for love, and deep inside his soul he knew Robin would be the woman to fill him.

O.J. knew nothing about Westchester so he began to research to find the popular spots to take Robin. He wanted to impress her and have a good time in doing so. He called the front desk of the hotel for a tour guide of Westchester. O.J. did his homework. He planned ahead for dinner reservations at a four-star restaurant, and then he phoned for a luxury rental car because he couldn't see picking up Robin with his work van. She had too much class for that. He wanted to escort her in style. He thought to himself *What would A.J. do if this was his date?* O.J. knew his brother's style and taste oh so well and always admired him for those qualities.

The Date

Time was getting close. It was 6 p.m. O.J. had showered, shaved and he had to remember to pick up the flowers he had ordered for Robin at the front desk. He was ready; he checked himself out in the full-length mirror. To his amazement, he was shocked at how much he looked like his twin brother. He thought he looked very debonair. For the final touch, a splash of cologne. *I hope she likes the fragrance*, he thought.

O.J. stopped at the front desk to pick up the bouquet of flowers. He noticed women's heads turning to watch as he exited the hotel. All he could think about was his brother A.J., because that's the kind of stares he often received from the ladies. He knew that he had it going on, which boosted his confidence level. He was ready for a night of romance. O.J. felt like he was on top of the world, and that he had deprived himself of feeling like a man for too long.

The air was brisk, but the night didn't seem cold to O.J. -- maybe because his heart had opened up to this beautiful woman. Overcoat across his arm, he rang the bell.

Robin opened the door. Knees shaking, she invited him in for a cocktail.

Robin smiled at him. "Good evening, Mr. O'Neil."

"Good evening, Ms. Jacobs. You look lovely."

"Thank you. You're looking suave yourself. Help yourself to a drink while I get my things," Robin pointed to the bar.

"These flowers are for you."

Robin reached for the flowers. "Thank you, O.J. They are absolutely beautiful. I'll put them in water."

"Beautiful flowers for a beautiful lady," O.J. eyed her.

Robin blushed and excused herself, went upstairs to get her purse and her coat. She went to her bedroom, took a deep breath and let out a sigh. She was thinking, *What a handsome man! He looks so good in that black suit, and those eyes -! He smells so good, too. I've got to get my composure together. OK, Robin, you can do this. Calm down, relax and act normal.*

Robin came down the stairs. O.J. was sipping a Coke; he never had been much of an alcohol drinker. He helped Robin with her coat, and off they went. The night air was cold and snowy. O.J. reached for Robin's hand and opened the car door. On the drive to the restaurant, they smiled like two kids with a crush on each other. When O.J. told her where they were going, Robin broke her silence.

"So we're dining at the Plaza Crown Royal tonight?"

"Nothing but the best for such a beautiful lady as yourself, Robin."

"Thank you, O.J. That's very sweet of you. In all my years in Westchester, I've never been to the Plaza Crown. I guess there's a first time for everything."

"Yes, indeed, first time for everything," O.J. said. "I can't remember how long it's been since I've dressed up in a suit or gone dancing or been in the presence of a beautiful woman like you."

Robin said, "Come now, O.J., I know better. A man as attractive as you has got to have women flying around him like flies."

O.J. blushed. "I've been so preoccupied with work, school and providing for my kids, there was never time for anyone or anything else."

Robin paused. "How many kids do you have?"

"Two. Nichole is 10, and Oscar Jr. is 21. I'll show you pictures when we get to the restaurant."

"What about their mom? Are the two of you still involved?" Robin asked.

O.J. was sweating bullets. He wanted to tell the truth, that he lived with the kid's mom, but that they had grown apart years ago. He wanted to be honest, but couldn't bring himself to tell her because he didn't want to ruin his chances of seeing her again.

"No, we're not involved, Robin." He said. "We grew apart years ago. We interact; keep in touch when it concerns the kids. I've been by myself for a long time. My kids have been my life."

Robin said, "I didn't mean to pry; it's just that you never know about people. It's hard for me to open up since my divorce, if you know what I mean."

"Robin, believe me I do understand so let's just enjoy our evening, dance a little and have some fun. I hope you're hungry."

Robin said, "As a matter a fact, I am." She was thinking, *Not the kind of hunger you're thinking of!*

They arrived at the restaurant. The lobby was like a grand ballroom with a huge fireplace. The atmosphere in the room was classy. The music playing was a soft jazz. The setting was very romantic. They were escorted to their table. A beautiful spray of flowers was arranged on the table, with candles surrounding it. O.J. comfortably pulled out Robin's chair and waited for her to be seated. His piercing dark brown eyes reflected the candlelight. Robin felt like a princess dining with her prince charming.

The waiter came over to start them off with drinks. Robin ordered a glass of wine to relax her. O.J. ordered a glass of tonic water with a twist of lemon. They gazed into each other's eyes. O.J. asked, "May I have this dance?"

The dance floor was crowded, but O.J. and Robin danced close, as if the room was theirs alone. Robin laid her head safely upon his broad chest. She felt a sense of security. O.J. held his arms around her tiny waist as if he had found a precious jewel. They were locked together in a feeling that they both longed for, the feeling that they were inseparable. They danced through song after song, forgetting about hunger. Their hunger was fulfilled with the affection they shared for each other.

"You're a wonderful dancer, Robin. And you smell delicious," O.J. cooed.

"Thank you. So do you."

They separated long enough to smile at each other. Luther Van dross' tune "Let Me Hold You Tight, if Only for One Night" was playing. O. J. began to hold Robin close, serenading her in her ear. Robin got weak as a wet noodle. She was so relaxed against his chest it was as if she was sleeping on a pillow. O.J. lifted her head, stared into her eyes with those dark brown eyes, and thanked her for going out with him.

"Robin, I really appreciate your being here with me. This is the best time I've had since I've been in Westchester. I'm so thankful to have met you."

Robin whispered, "I'm having a great time too, Lightfoot."

They both laughed. "Shall we order dinner, Ms. Jacobs? No one is dancing but us."

Robin said, "Yes, we shall, Mr. O'Neil. Time flies when you're having fun."

O.J. led her back to their table. They dined on a fine meal and talked until closing time. Everyone had left except for the kitchen staff, and they were still talking.

O.J. said, "Robin, I think we'd better be making moves; looks like we're the last to leave. I'm going to take care of the check and get the car warm. You wait in the lobby by the fireplace. I'll come back for you."

O.J. made his exit to the car. Robin sat mesmerized by the glowing fire. She kept thinking, *Where has this man been all my life? He's a perfect gentleman, and an excellent entertainer and dancer.* She was deep in thought when O.J. whispered her name. "Robin, honey, the car is ready."

Robin didn't want what felt like a perfect night to end. She decided she would suggest they drive to Highland Falls, a park with high mountains which overlooked the city. She thought it would be a nice sight to show him, the night scenery of Westchester.

As they drove, Robin said, "O.J., dinner was lovely. Thank you."

"You're very welcome."

"I have an idea," Robin said. "Why don't I show you the night scenery? We can drive to Highland Falls. It's beautiful at night."

"Just lead the way. The night is still young," O.J. said.

They arrived at Highland Falls; the view of the city was breathtaking. The moon was bright.

"Robin, this is unbelievable; how beautiful! It's like we're up in an airplane, the lights look so tiny. I had no idea that Westchester was this big."

Robin said, "I used to ride up here all the time after my dad died to collect my thoughts."

"I'm sorry you lost your dad. Mine left us when we were kids. My mom raised us kids alone. Now she passed away."

"How sad! O.J., I'm sorry."

"I was only 13 when my mom passed. My grandmother took us in and cared for us. I loved Big Momma, but she was nothing like mom. My mom worked so hard it killed her. She had a heart attack; my dad leaving her with three kids was rough on her. That's why I vowed to always be there for my kids. I don't want to do to them what my dad did to us. He didn't want us."

Robin said, "I'm sorry." She felt his pain. She reached for his hands to let him know, *I feel you're hurt. I know your loss. I recognize those feelings.* O.J. apologized for the emotions he displayed.

"Robin, forgive me; it all seems like yesterday. You just never get over it."

"Don't apologize," Robin said. "I understand. I haven't cried a tear since the day my dad was pronounced dead. I can't remember a single tear on that very day, and I've buried the rest along with him. It just builds up on the inside. One day I'll break; one day it will come out. But I had to be strong, O.J. I had to keep my family together."

"Robin, you're a strong woman. I'm a man, but even I cried when my mother died, and I still cry. Come here let me hold you. Please let me hold you. It's OK. You're safe with me. You're safe to cry, you're safe to scream, but let it go, baby, let go. Let me hold you."

O.J. couldn't believe the emotion in own his voice. It wasn't an emotion of a romantic gesture, but that of empathy and caring. He felt Robin's pain. He wanted her to let all those bottled up feelings go. He wanted to be the one to open her heart. Robin, feeling very secure with him, laid her head on his shoulder, and before she knew it the tears began to flow like a river. She was crying uncontrollably. O.J. held her so tight; he rocked her like a baby. Soothing her, caressing her. *It's OK; I'm here for you Robin, it's OK.* He took his handkerchief from his jacket pocket and wiped the tears from her face.

From out of the glove compartment, he took a small pamphlet. He placed it in Robin's hands. It was a Biblical scripture which read "Weeping may endure for a night, but Joy comes in the morning." Psalm 30:5

Robin looked at the words, and O.J. recited them to her with hope in his eyes.

"It's OK, Robin. Take this scripture and believe in your heart that your dad and my mom are resting in the Lord. It's OK to cry; even Jesus wept. Please keep these words, and know that life will bring you sorrow, but it also brings great joy.

Robin looked at him with amazement. No one had ever given her such comforting words. She knew then that there was something special about him.

"O.J. you're so kind and thoughtful for a guy. I needed to hear those words, and I'll always remember you for such encouraging advice. You're something else. Thank you." She kissed him on the cheek.

"Robin, keep those words with you whenever you feel like shedding a tear. Know that God is in control and joy does follow sadness. After all, I met you."

Robin looked into his eyes; she saw the seriousness on his face. She said, "I'm glad I met you, too, O.J."

They caressed each other, hugged and looked out into the moonlit night. The moon was bright, the snow sparkled, and love was in the air.

Finally O.J. said, "I'd better get you home. I don't want to overextend my welcome. It's been an interesting night for us both. Robin, I hope you enjoyed yourself and we can see each other again."

"O.J. I haven't ever laughed and cried so much in one night. Thank you so much for a lovely date. Yes, I'd love to see you again."

On the drive home, Robin was very relaxed. She laid her head to rest on his shoulder as her prince escorted her home safely. O.J. walked her to the door. They kissed so passionately they forgot about the cold. The kiss was warm, gentle, and lingered until they both let go. Staring into each other's eyes, they both said at the same time, "Good night." O.J. took the keys from her hand, unlocked the door and waited until she was inside.

"Thank you, Robin, for such a memorable night. Please see me tomorrow."

"I will. I'll call you."

"OK, good night. Now lock up until tomorrow." He blew a kiss.

"Good night, Mr. O'Neil," Robin said as she closed the door. O.J. stood there with a grin on his face until he heard the lock and saw the upstairs light go on. He wanted to be sure she was safely inside. He walked back to the car with a burst of energy, nothing but Robin on his mind and the scent of her perfume on his jacket. He felt like a new man, like he had won the lottery. O.J. realized that he had been missing out on feelings. He knew from their date that he could care for someone again. What he shared with the woman at home was dead, but Robin gave him a feeling of life. As he drove to his hotel room, he kept thinking about seeing her tomorrow. How he couldn't wait to see her lovely face again, her smile, and hold her in his arms once more.

Robin dressed for bed. As she hung up her attire, she got a sniff of O.J.'s cologne. She sniffed her blouse just to reflect on how close he had held her when they danced. Robin hung up her outfit, got on her knees and began to pray. *God, thank you for a beautiful date, thank you for allowing me to meet O.J. Thank you for such inspirational words. Lord, I'm scared to love. Help me, guide me, Lord. Amen.*

Robin felt the need to confess her feeling before her Creator. It was O.J. who had steered her back in the direction in which she was raised. It was his comforting scripture that led her back to her Heavenly Father.

Robin couldn't wait to see O.J. again. He made her feel special. She realized, *With this man I can be me and show my emotions.* That's what she had always wanted in a mate. Not only did he have good looks, he had emotion. Robin knew she had to see him again. Until tomorrow.

The Next Day

She was sound asleep when the phone rang. The answering machine picked it up before she could. It was Ellen. "Robin, if you're there, pick up. I want to know what happened last night. Girl, wake up. Or maybe you have company, and I should leave you alone. Wake up!"

Robin picked up the phone. It was 6 a.m. "Ellen, do you know what time it is?"

Ellen said, "Yes, I do. It's time for you to wake up and tell me how the date went. I'm at work, and I can't get started until you tell me."

Robin, wiping the sleep from her eyes, sat up in the bed. Just speaking O.J.'s name gave her a burst of energy.

"Ellen, girl, let me tell you, I've never met anyone like him. We dined in style. He picked me up on time, looking handsome as ever and smelling real good. He brought flowers, girl. He took me to the Crown Royal. We danced half the night. The food was excellent. We left there and went to Highland Falls. Ellen, it was so romantic. He's a perfect gentleman. I really had a good time."

"Robin, that's good. Did he kiss you good night?"

"Girl, did he. I was elevated above heaven, if there's any such place. He's a fantastic kisser. He's special."

Ellen said, "Girl, I can hear it all in your voice. Are you guys going out again?"

Robin said, "I would hope so. I'm going to call him today."

Ellen said, "Robin, you need this. I'm so excited for you. Just take it slow. Listen, I better start my day. I've got a 7 a.m. meeting. I'll buzz you later. If Mr. O'Neil doesn't make plans with you, maybe we can take in a movie."

Robin said, "Sounds good. Talk to you later."

The phone rang again. Robin said, "Hello?"

It was Larry. "Hi, Mom. How you doing?"

"I'm fine, son. How are you?"

Larry said, "I'm good. Listen, Mom, I won't be coming home for spring break. I met a girl, and she invited me for dinner to meet her folks. Mom, please understand."

"Larry, you know how important it is for the family to be together. I planned a dinner for you. What would the party be without you? Honey, I understand meeting someone and wanting to spend time with that person, but nothing or no one takes the place of family."

Larry said, "Mom, I'm sorry. You're right. I didn't mean to upset you. I'll be home for spring break. Maybe Angela can arrange for me to meet her parents some other time. Mom, I know how much it means to you, the family being together. How is Grandmother?"

"Honey, she's fine. Listen, tell me about Angela. It sounds a little serious. Your meeting her folks and all," Robin said.

"Mom, she's smart and pretty. I wouldn't say it's serious, but we are seeing each other on the regular. We study together. Mom, she's a bio major. She knows her stuff. I'd like for her to one day meet you. I tell her all the time, my mom is the rock in my life. I tell Angela you keep me on the straight and narrow, and that I want to make you proud of me."

"Honey, you've made me the proudest and happiest mom on this earth. I love you and want what's best for you. For now, it's an education. I'd love to meet Angela one day; she sounds like a nice young lady."

"Mom, I believe you'd like her. So it's settled; I'm home for spring break. Oh, and Mom, say hello to Ellen for me, and tell her the goodies were right on time."

"I'll do that baby. Do you have enough winter gear?" Robin asked.

"Mom, I'm fine. I miss you."

"I miss you too, sweetheart. "

"Have you been keeping yourself busy? How are your classes coming along?" Larry asked.

"Honey, I've got a lot on my plate these days. Classes are hectic. I'm trying to maintain my 3.0 average. Gonna be tough this quarter, but I'm determined."

"That's my mom! Guess what?"

"What, honey?"

"I'm a chip off the old block; my average is running high this quarter. I've aced every test so far."

"See, Larry, how can I not be proud? I love you so much."

"I love you too, Mom. I'd better get to class. Listen, don't worry; I'll be home for spring break. I'll call you next weekend. Love you, Mom. Later."

"Love you too, son. Be good."

The phone rang a third time. It was O.J. "Good morning, Ms. Jacobs. How are you?"

"Good morning, Mr. O'Neil. I'm fine, thank you. How are you?"

"I'm good, Robin. I really enjoyed myself last night. How about meeting me for lunch?"

"O.J., that's really sweet of you, but you don't have to do that."

O.J. cut in. "I don't have to, but I want to see you today – soon!"

Robin admired his persistence. She also wanted to see him. "How's 12:30?" she asked.

O.J. said, "That's fine. I'm on call. Hope you don't mind if we're interrupted."

"Believe me, it's not a problem. I do understand when duty calls."

"Robin, would you mind if we met at the restaurant? I'm all over the city today. It would be easier if you decide on a place, page me with your decision, and I'll meet you there."

Robin said, "Not a problem at all, O.J. I understand."

"Thank you. Oh, and Robin, I'm in uniform today, so please excuse my attire. It won't be anything like last night."

Robin laughed. "O.J., it's cool. I understand. You're working. It's 9 a.m. now so let's say I page you within the hour with the details."

"Sounds like a plan. Until then."

"Later, Mr. O'Neil," Robin said and hung up the phone.

A Picnic at the Pier

She looked through her wardrobe to see what she could wear. She wanted to look radiant for O.J. She decided on her tight purple sweater with the low neck-line and a pair of fitted jeans. She wanted to be comfortable and not overdressed, since he was dressed in work attire.

Robin couldn't decide where to meet for lunch. *I know the best food joint in Westchester,* she thought to herself. *Robin's kitchen. I'll fix a basket lunch for us, and we can picnic in the van.* Robin decided what she should prepare. She made herself very busy in the kitchen. She made her family's secret chicken salad recipe on rye bread, and she filled the thermos with hot vegetable soup. She cut fresh fruit for dessert. She made a thermos full of coffee just the way O.J. liked it. She packed the basket with her fine tablecloth, silverware and a freshly cut rose.

There, lunch is ready to be served. Time flew; she hadn't paged O.J. since she'd gotten so caught up in preparing the meal she had let time slip by. *I'd better page him; he's probably thinking the worst.* She paged him. Within minutes he phoned back.

"Robin, I thought you had forgotten me. I figured something came up."

Robin said, "As a matter of fact, it did."

O.J. was silent. She wondered if he was disappointed. She said, "O.J., are you there?"

"I'm here, Robin. I wanted so badly to see you today, but if you've got other plans, believe me, it's OK."

Robin laughed. "I'm not letting you off the hook that easy. Yes, I do have other plans and they include you."

She imagined O.J. smiling, just from the way his voice changed. "Oh, is that a fact, Ms. Jacobs?"

Robin said, "Yes, it is, Mr. O'Neil. We're having lunch in your work van."

"In my van," O.J. repeated. "You mean stop and go at some fast food place?"

Robin laughed. "No, silly. I've prepared lunch, and we're having a picnic in the dead of winter. In the back of your van. How's that for style?"

Now it was O.J.'s turn to laugh. "Woman, you're incredible. I'm flattered. Where shall we meet?"

Robin said, "Are you familiar with the Lake Street Pier? It's north of the hotel you're staying in downtown."

"Yes, I know the spot. Call the time and I'll be there."

"Let's keep it at 12:30," Robin said.

"12:30 it is. I'll be there and, Robin, drive safely. You might want to wear an extra sweater since it's really cold today."

"O.J. you're just not used to this Westchester cold. Florida has thinned your blood."

"OK, OK you're right. I can't adjust to the cold, but I want you safe and warm."

Robin said, "OK, Mr. O'Neil, let me get dressed so that I can meet on time."

"See you soon, Robin."

"Later."

O.J. was stuck in traffic on the other side of town; quit a distance from the pier. It was 11 a.m., and the dispatcher had just called him to go on a job. O.J. looked at the time and the traffic. He was trying to figure out how he could turn down this next job so it wouldn't interfere with his plans to meet Robin. He got off the highway at the next exit, pulled over and put the van in park.

He phoned his roommate Sam. Sam had the day off, but he wanted to make some extra money. O.J. felt that Sam was qualified to do the job; besides the dispatcher wouldn't know as long as someone showed up at the residence. He phoned Sam back at the hotel.

"Hello, Sam. It's O.J."

"Hey, man, busy day or what?"

O.J. said, "Yes, it is, as a matter of fact -- that's why I'm calling. I've got more runs today than I can handle. Can you help me out?"

Sam said, "Sure can, man. I need the hours."

O.J. said, "Great! Dispatcher says the hot water tank at this residence isn't working properly. The call came in about 15 minutes ago. The address is 131 Oakland Drive. They're expecting someone within the hour."

Sam jotted the information down. "I'm on it. 131 Oakland Drive?"

"That's it. Thanks man," O.J. said.

Sam said, "Thank you, O.J. Oh and by the way, your brother left a message. He said for you to contact him. Nothing urgent."

O.J. said, "OK, thanks. Later."

He let out a sigh of relief. The only thing he had to deal with now was the traffic. He wanted to get there before Robin, so that he could clean out the back of the van, make it presentable for her and give them sit-down room. O.J. made his way through the traffic. The roads were slippery, covered with snow, and the cars were bumper to bumper. He couldn't get used to driving in the snow. Everything was slow motion, especially making his way to the woman who made him feel so alive. O.J. felt as if he was in a funeral procession. Steadily blowing his horn for cars to move along helped to relieve some frustration. He didn't want anything to hinder him from getting to Robin.

It was 11:30 and he was closer to the pier. O.J. wanted to stop at a florist to get Robin a flower. Downtown Westchester was busy for a Saturday. Seemed like the whole town had one thing in mind today, shopping. Circling the area for a parking spot, he located a floral shop. O.J. quickly drove into the parking space, the van slipping and sliding from side to side. He accelerated the gas too hard, which caused the van to glide.

At last he found a space, put the van in park, added coins to the parking meter and went inside to see what flower he'd buy for his rose, Robin. He thought he'd phone Robin again to tell her to drive slowly and safely. He wanted to suggest maybe he should come to her place. He was thinking of her safety, and he knew how bad the traffic was. He didn't want to ruin her idea of a picnic; besides he was looking forward to it. It sounded so romantic to him. He gave her a buzz from his cell phone, and found himself listening to her answering machine. "Hello, you've reached the Jacobs residence. Please leave a message, thank you."

O.J. hung up when he heard the machine. He was feeling anxious and nervous; he wanted so badly to see Robin, but he wanted her safe. He proceeded inside the flower shop. His pager beeped. It was the dispatcher calling. He had to phone in.

"Hello," he said. "This is badge #234. Oscar O'Neil returning the call."

The dispatcher said, "O'Neil, there's been an emergency call concerning the residence at 131 Oakland Drive. Apparently there's a gas leak in the house. The fire department called to tell us not to report there for our own safety. If you're en route to the location, cancel your run. The family had to evacuate the premises, and I'm instructed to tell you not to go there. The fire department is at the scene. They're avoiding a possible explosion."

O.J. was sweating and nervous. "I was en route to the location. I'll stand by for further instructions. Thanks."

"Very good," the dispatcher said. "Thank God I stopped you, and you're safe."

O.J., in a panic, hurried and got the dispatcher off the phone. He had to contact Sam right away. Putting his thoughts of Robin on hold, he realized he had to act quickly. He phoned Sam at the hotel; there was no answer. Panicked, he searched through his wallet for a list of pager numbers which included Sam's. Dropping his wallet to the floor, he picked up the contents. Out of his wallet fell a picture of his kids.

All O.J. could think of at that moment was Sam and his family. What would his family do if something terrible happened? It would be his fault. How could he explain his asking Sam to cover for him? O.J. was petrified. Where had he put those pager numbers?

The Blizzard

He realized that he'd put the pager numbers in the glove compartment of the van, so he rushed to the van. Within those few minutes, the weather took a turn for the worse. Visibility was terrible due to the high wind. O.J. met his first blizzard. He couldn't see his way to the van. Finally he located it, and it was completely covered with snow. His mind was shifting back and forth, worrying about Robin traveling in the blizzard. Once inside the van, he tore open the glove compartment and pushed everything to the floor. He scrambled through the mess and found the list of numbers. Immediately he paged Sam from his cell phone. He entered 911 emergency code for Sam to return the call. O.J. sat anxiously waiting; after a few minutes of waiting there was no response. O.J. didn't feel the temperature of the cold weather. Instead he was sweating, hot and nervous. He paged Sam a second time. Please, Sam, he thought, answer the page. Please Lord help me. Finally his cell phone rang.

O.J. thought, *Sam, please let this be you.*

It was. "O.J., man, it's me, I'm stuck in traffic on the expressway. Visibility is so bad, I can barely see. I'm trying to make it to Oakland Drive. The reception is bad due to the weather; my cell phone was dead for a while."

O.J. said, "Man, thank God you're safe! Listen, don't go to Oakland Drive. Dispatch called; there's an emergency gas leak, which could cause an explosion. The fire department is there now. Thank God for bad weather."

Sam said, "I know. God saved me between the blizzard and the traffic. If this blizzard hadn't started, I would have been there by now. Thanks for calling me. I'm going to make my way back to the hotel."

O.J. said, "Man, that was a close call. My heart was racing. I'm so glad you're safe. Drive safe, OK? I'll see you later tonight. Sam, thanks for being there for me."

"Yeah, O.J., you drive safe. The wind is getting worse out, so be careful. Talk at you later."

O.J., wiping the sweat away, thanked God that Sam was safe. He had no way of contacting Robin. He didn't have a cell number for her so he hurried to get to the pier. In the vicinity of the pier, he noticed cars pulled over on the side of the road due to the hazardous driving. He could barely make out the sign "Lake Street Pier." O.J. turned into the parking lot. The pier was deserted, neither a person in sight nor a single boat.

He left the van running and got out to brush the snow off. It was so cold that when he opened the back of the van, the doors were frozen stiff. He glanced at his watch. It was 12:45. O.J. began to pace back and forth. He didn't see or hear a car approaching the lot. His mind began to wander. Maybe Robin got into an accident, maybe she was stuck on the side of the road somewhere, or maybe she was stranded in the freezing cold.

O.J. stood outside the van, looking in every direction. He noticed a car coming his way. He heaved a sigh of relief. It was Robin. She was driving about five miles per hour. O.J. ran to her car, waving both hands for her to stop.

"Robin, are you OK?" He squeezed her tightly. He was so relieved to see her.

Robin said, "I'm fine, O.J. I didn't realize how bad the weather was. I traveled too far to turn back. I took my time."

"Get back in the car. I'll drive you to the van, and from there I'm taking you home. We can pick your car up later after the blizzard dies down. Better yet, I'll get one of the guys to trail me, and I'll drive your car home safely. I'm not taking 'no' for an answer."

Robin realized she couldn't argue with a protective man. She followed O.J. to the van. He carried the basket lunch. O.J. had had enough excitement for one day. He wanted to be sure Robin was home safe, so he drove her himself. On the drive to Robin's house, they passed many cars pulled over to the side of the road, and still the snow fell steadily.

O.J. drove very slowly; it gave him time to talk with Robin. It took them two hours to get to her house. In normal driving conditions, it would have only been an hour. O.J. pulled into Robin's snow-covered driveway. He escorted her to the door and then told her to go inside and warm up while he shoveled the driveway.

Robin didn't argue with him; she went inside and made a fresh pot of coffee. Next she spread the tablecloth on the living room floor. Robin was persistent; she was determined to have their picnic. She heated the vegetable soup and unpacked the basket. O.J. made his way into the house. He was drenched in snow, and his clothes were soaking wet.

"O.J., you're soaking wet," Robin said. "Get out of those clothes, and let me dry them for you. You'll catch your death of cold. I'll get you something of my sons to wear until your clothes are dry."

"Thank you, Robin. I am chilled to the bone."

Robin went upstairs to Larry's room. She found a pair of jeans and a sweatshirt. They would do for now. She came back downstairs, gave them to O.J., and showed him to the bathroom where he could get cleaned up and then they would eat. O.J. went upstairs to change clothes. Robin sat in the living room, waiting for him to bring the wet clothes down.

O.J. came downstairs. "I feel better now. Thank you, Robin."

Robin said, "You're welcome. Are those clothes comfortable for you? I can give you a bathrobe."

"I'm fine, Robin. Here are my wet clothes."

"Do you mind if I wash them?"

O.J. didn't care; that would give him more time to spend with her.

"No, not at all," he said. "How about I start a fire in the fireplace while you're working on the clothes?"

"Great! Let me make you a cup of coffee. You've got to be cold, and I know how you like your coffee. Black and sweet."

O.J. laughed. "Yeah, just like you." They both smiled.

Robin made her way to the kitchen. She couldn't get over how masculine and fit O.J. looked in Larry's jeans. His protectiveness and his physique turned her on. He was well formed. She gave him the coffee. As he was placing the logs on the fire, she couldn't help but notice his nice, round proportioned ass. He was built. Robin hurried to the laundry room to keep her composure together.

When she came back to the living room, O.J. was lying in front of the fireplace, his body stretched, all masculine curves.

Robin said, "The fire looks cozy, O.J. Your clothes are in the wash."

"Robin," he said, "come sit with me."

Robin moved to his side. She gazed into the firelight in O.J.'s eyes. He reached for her hand and took her to the tablecloth where she had neatly arranged the food.

"Let me serve you, my dear," O.J. said. "Everything looks delicious."

Robin had a spread fit for a king. The setting was romantic. O.J. dimmed the lights. The reflection from the fireplace lit the room. They sat on the floor, comfortable, gazing at each other; neither of them had food on their mind. O.J. brought the chicken salad to

Robin's mouth, and then he took a bite from the same side of the sandwich. He began feeding her like she was his sweet baby.

Robin, speechless, mouth full, adored the attention. Gazing into his eyes, she wanted to kiss him at that very moment. O.J. moved closer to her. Without a word said, he lifted her chin and slowly kissed her. It was as if he had read her mind. Robin, overcome with emotion, let herself go into the arms of her protector. She immediately pushed back, wanting to maintain control.

"I'd better go check on the laundry," she said.

She was running away from the feeling. She was afraid to give in to what she felt for O.J. O.J. was feeling it too; he'd forgotten about his situation in Florida. He wanted Robin in every way. He felt life had been brought back into his dead soul. O.J. sat thinking, should he tell her his secret and risk not seeing her again? Robin came back into the room and noticed the look on his face.

"O.J., is there something you want to say? The look on your face is so serious. A penny for your thoughts."

"Robin, listen to what I'm about to say, and please don't take it the wrong way…"

Robin sat very quiet wondering what was on his mind.

"Robin, before I met you, life was dull. I made my children my life. I filled my life with work. I had forgotten what it was like to hold a woman, care for her, and want her. You restored those feelings again. Never have I felt this way for any woman. I wish we had met at a different time in our lives. Forgive me for my forwardness, but this is how I feel about you. I want to continue seeing you until I go back to Florida."

Robin sat in amazement, not knowing what to say. She felt the same way about him. Their feelings were mutual. After the divorce, she had buried herself in work and school. Oscar O'Neil was the best thing that had happened to her in years.

Now she said, "O.J., I've been hurt. Please understand I'm afraid to let my feelings go, afraid to love. My heart can't bear another heartache."

O.J. reached for her hand to hold. "Robin, I would never hurt you. I care about you. Trust me, please. Just let me show you. Let's take it day by day."

"My ex-husband was the last man who told me to trust him, and it almost destroyed me."

"I'm not your ex. Robin, look me in the eye and tell me you don't feel what I feel, and I'll walk out of this house never to bother you again."

Robin turned away; she couldn't avoid the feeling. O.J. took her in his arms and held her close. He caressed her long black shoulder-length hair. He reassured her that her feelings were safe with him. In the back of his mind he knew he had to keep his secret if he wanted to keep her.

They kissed passionately. O.J. unbuttoned her sweater; he succulently kissed her breast. Robin was in ecstasy; too weak to resist, she gave in to the passion. They moved in slow motion as if they were waltzing, each stroke penetrating, fire slowly burning. They made love until they both lay in exhaustion, their naked bodies in sweat-drenched closeness.

They lay in front of the fire, exposed in their nakedness, O.J. holding Robin tight in his arms as if he never wanted to let her go. They had forgotten about eating; the food was secondary. O.J. was steadily kissing Robin as if she was something delectable to eat. The lovemaking was sensual, and they played most of the night, finally drifting off to sleep in each other's arms.

Snowed In

O.J. awakened in the middle of the night. The fire was still smoldering, but it was a bit drafty in the room. He stared down at his princess, worrying about his secret. Then he tiptoed out of the room so as not to wake Robin. He searched for a blanket to cover her.

He gently placed the blanket over her and then he restarted the fire, putting more logs on to burn. He went to the window to check the weather. Gazing into the night, all he could see was snow covering everything. The van was completely covered. They were snowed in.

Silently he made his way to the kitchen to put the food away. Careful not to wake Robin, he turned on the TV in the kitchen to listen to the weather report. The TV flashed a weather advisory telling people not to travel in the blizzard. It was expected to last 24 hours. O.J. couldn't think of anywhere else he'd rather be. He peeked in on Robin. She was sleeping like a baby. He thought he'd check his cell phone messages. There were three messages on his phone.

Message#1: "Hi, Dad, Oscar Jr. We heard the weather is really bad up that way. Mom and Nichole wanted to talk. Hope you're OK. Please call us back when you get this message. We're all doing fine. Love you, Dad."

Message#2: "Hey, O.J., man, it's A.J. Just checking to make sure everything went OK with your date. I'm leaving for Los Angeles this afternoon, got business there. I'll be gone a few days. Checked in on the family; everybody is good. Call me on my cell, man, when you stop romancing. Keepin' it real with you, bro. Have a good time; you deserve it. Holla back at me, man."

Message#3: O.J., it's Samone. You should have called by now. The kids and I are worried sick. The blizzard has caused a state of emergency. It's all over the news here. Nichole is crying for her daddy. Call us as soon as you can. I hear a lot of the phone lines are dead. We love you."

O.J. panicked when he heard Samone's voice. He had to call home to ease their worries, and let them know he was safe. He didn't want to chance Robin's waking up and hearing him talk to Samone. He peeked in on Robin, she was still asleep. It was breaking daylight, and the snow was still falling. O.J. went to the laundry room and put his clothes in the dryer. He thought he better check on Sam so he called the hotel. The phone line was dead. He couldn't even get a signal on his cell phone.

He picked up the phone in Robin's laundry room; it was dead, too. He made his way back upstairs and thought he'd make fresh coffee. O.J. worried about calling home. He had to reach Sam to let him know he was safe and to relay the message to his family if they called the hotel. He was going to tell Sam he had been dispatched to a residence, and the family was nice enough to care for him during the blizzard.

He kept trying the hotel. Still no outgoing dial tone. He didn't like the idea of putting Sam in the middle of his confusion, but he had to make sure he covered all bases, plus he wanted to make sure his family didn't worry.

O.J. finally got through to the hotel from the cell phone.

"Holiday Inn, may I help you?"

O.J. said, "Room #1101, please. Thank you."

"Hello?"

"Sam, hey it's O.J."

"Man, are you all right? Where you been? Are you stranded?"

O.J. said, "Sam, I'm fine. I got dispatched to a residence right after we talked. The blizzard was so bad the family was nice enough to let me camp out until the weather eases up."

Sam said, "I know, man. People are stuck everywhere. A state of emergency has been called. I'm glad you're OK. That was decent of that family. Speaking of family, yours called several times. I told your son I'm sure he had nothing to worry about."

O.J. said, "Sam, you're a lifesaver. I owe you big-time, man. Listen, if my family calls back, pass on the information I gave you. Let them know my cell phone is down. I'm fine, and I'll contact them as soon as I can."

Sam said, "Will do. O.J., don't worry; I'll make sure to ease their worries. Call me if you need me for anything."

"Thanks, Sam. Once the weather breaks in a few days, I may need you to help trail a friend's car that got stuck in the blizzard."

Sam said, "Not a problem. Take care, O.J."

O.J. went back into the living room to check on Robin; she was still sleeping. He sat in front of the burning fire. O.J.'s thoughts were in Florida, wondering how he could have remained in a dead relationship for so long. Being with Robin made him feel so alive. O.J. knew in his heart he felt very deeply for Robin. He also knew that the time would come when he'd have to tell her about Samone. He slowly approached Robin and kissed her on the forehead.

Robin opened her eyes. "Good morning, Mr. O'Neil," she said smiling up at him.

"Good morning, sweetheart. How did you sleep?"

"Very well. Thanks to you."

O.J. took Robin in his arms, held her very tight and whispered in her ear, "I think I'm falling in love with you. You're the most beautiful woman I've ever had in my life. You give me a new reason for living. You've brought happiness into my heart. How can I leave Westchester without you, Robin?"

"O.J., I think you're wonderful, too. Kiss me, take me."

They began to make love again, both expressing heartfelt feelings. O.J. blocked out all thoughts of never seeing Robin again. They lay in each other's arms in front of the fire.

After a long time, Robin said, "Do you realize we're snowed in?"

"I can't think of anywhere in the world I'd rather be right now but in your arms. In fact, when I leave to go back to Florida, if I send for you, will you come?"

Robin sighed. "Yes, O.J. I'll come." She hugged him very close. "Now, how about something to eat?"

"That sounds good, but I'm doing the cooking. I make a serious omelet. You relax, and I'll make breakfast."

"You cook?" She smiled.

"Yes, I cook. I'm going to take care of you today, Ms. Jacobs. Your every wish is my command."

Robin said, "Then kiss me."

O.J. kissed her. They both were like wild animals craving each other.

"I'm going to shower while you're in the kitchen cooking."

"Take your time," he told her. "I got this."

Robin made her way upstairs. O.J. went into the kitchen. He wanted a moment alone so he could try calling Florida again. Using his cell phone, the number was ringing. He peeked his head around the kitchen door to listen for the shower running.

Samone picked up. "Hello?"

O.J. said, "Hi, Samone. It's me. Where are the kids?"

"O.J., are you all right? We've been worried sick."

"I'm fine, Samone. The weather is really bad here. A customer was nice enough to put me up. We got snowed in."

Samone said. "That was very nice of them. We called the hotel several times. Sam told us you were safe. The kids and I have been watching the Weather Channel all day. Nichole was so worried."

"Samone, I'm sorry. I'd have called sooner if I could. I was just missing the kids. Are they OK?

"Oh, so you don't miss me?"

"Samone, look, I didn't call to argue. Please let me speak to the kids."

After O.J. talked to the kids, he felt relieved. He got off the phone before Robin came down.

He felt so torn. Things were happening so fast. He had finally met the woman of his dreams. He had a family in Florida, and he'd soon have to leave his soul mate behind with miles of distance between them. O.J.'s head began to ache. Too much to think about for right now. This situation was definitely a peace ground discussion; he felt the need to talk to his brother. O.J. listened for Robin and heard her singing in the shower. Wow, she had a nice voice -- she sang like an angel, his angel. She sounded very happy.

O.J. called his brother. He needed to hear his voice and get some reassurance.

He got the answering machine. "Yes, you dialed right. This is A.J., and apparently I'm busy. So please leave a message and I'll fit you in. If this is an emergency, hit me on my pager #720-9197."

O.J. left a message on A.J's voice mail. "Hey, man, so you're in L.A.? Man, things are good. I think I love this woman. A.J., she's everything I ever dreamed of. I'm stuck in a blizzard at her house and loving every minute of it. Man, I got a situation. Need to talk with

121

you, bro. Listen, you be safe in L.A. Hit me back on my cell when you get this message. A.J., man, she's the one. Peace."

O.J. began preparing breakfast. He set the table, complete with candles burning. He was a good cook and loved to do it. He couldn't remember the last time he'd prepared breakfast for Samone. He and Samone had grown up together; they were kids when they met. Samone had gotten pregnant, and he remained in the relationship to do the honorable thing, to be a man.

He felt obligated to Samone and the kids. Never had he loved her in the way he felt for Robin in such a short period of time. O.J. realized that he had just settled for less, and thought about how much happiness he had missed out on. He knew he wanted to see Robin again once he left Westchester. What was he to do? How could he keep his secret? He didn't want to keep Robin in the dark, but he didn't want to lose her either. He only had a few weeks left in Westchester, and he wanted to spend as much time as he could with Robin. It was as if his heart had opened up to her.

Breakfast was ready and smelled delicious. O.J. cooked a stuffed omelet with all kinds of fresh veggies Robin had in the fridge. He waited for her to come downstairs and placed a towel over his arm like a waiter.

"Baby, it smells so good! And look at this table! I'm impressed; a girl could get used to this treatment."

Pulling out her chair, O.J. announced, "Ms. Jacobs, I'll be your server. Please be seated. May I start you off with coffee?"

Robin was smiling, loving the attention. "Coffee would be nice. I'm going to have to give you a big tip."

O.J. served her with pleasure. Then he sat across from her, watching her eat.

"Robin," he said, "you're beautiful early in the morning. I hope you know how much I enjoyed you last night." He reached for her hand.

"O.J., you're incredible, and a good cook, too. You know, I could get used to this. You'll be leaving in a few weeks. I'm going to miss you."

"Babe, I'll be a call away, and I'm going to send for you. Robin, I need you in my life. You've given me happiness. I know it's premature to be talking this way, but do you believe in love at first sight?"

"Yes, I do, O.J., and I'm feelin' you, too. The distance between us is so far but, like you said, we can call each other. See one another when we have time."

O.J. said, "Honey, I promise not to let you go. You're here now." He patted his heart. "Let's not worry about tomorrow; let's enjoy the time we have left. Eat your food before it gets cold."

Neither of them was concerned with the blizzard; all that mattered to them was that they were together. They finished breakfast, and then cleaned up the kitchen. Robin pulled out her photo album and showed O.J. pictures of her family.

"Maybe one day you'll get a chance to meet my family," she said.

O.J. said, "Yes, I believe that will happen, and you'll have a chance to meet mine."

The remainder of the day, they talked, getting to know each other. O.J. was snowed in with Robin for two whole days. They both blocked out the world and enjoyed one another.

The after-effects from the blizzard slowed everything down. Even though the blizzard had started on a Saturday, businesses and schools were closed for two more days. Neither of them had to go to work. They were as excited as the kids were, having that time to be with each other. They exhausted each other with lovemaking.

Finally Robin said, "Since you've only got a few weeks left in Westchester, why don't you stay with me until you leave? I'll make your life nice and cozy here at my house. You're more than welcome and I'd love to have you."

"Thank you, Robin, I appreciate the offer, but I don't want to impose. But if you will allow me to, I'd like to see you every chance I get before I have to go."

"You've got a date, Mr. O'Neil."

A FEW WEEKS LATER

"Robin, girl, I don't hear much from you these days. Dating hot and heavy?" It was Ellen.

"Ellen, forgive me. O.J. and I have built something strong within these past few weeks. My honey leaves me tomorrow. Tonight we're celebrating, going back to the Crown Plaza where we had our first date. Ellen, how do I say good-bye to the man I love?"

"Robin, maybe it's not good-bye, but hello. Somebody has got to relocate. How are the two of you going to handle the distance?"

"For now we'll commute, visit one another whenever we can. I'll visit Florida soon."

"Robin, you know you can lean on me if you need to talk. I'm sure you guys will work through the distance."

"You're right. Neither of us can let this go," Robin assured herself.

"Just look your best tonight. Enjoy your last evening together. Will you be taking him to the airport?"

"Yes. His flight is at 6 a.m., so we'll have dinner and turn in early. He's going to bring his things with him when he picks me up tonight for dinner."

"Girl, stop worrying. You know that man is not going to leave here with you all down and depressed. Cheer up, enjoy him. Look forward to the next time."

"I know, Ellen. Let me get dressed. I may need you tomorrow, girl, so listen for me."

"You know I got your back, Robin. Have a good time and don't worry."

"Thanks, Ellen. Love you."

"Love you too, girl; chin up. Talk at you soon."

Dinner at the Crown Royal

O.J. wiped the tears from Robin's face. "Robin, look at me. Please don't cry. Once I get to Florida, I promise you in a few weeks I'll be sending for you."

Luther Van dross' song "Here and Now" played in the background.

O.J. immediately took Robin's hand, led her to the dance floor where they had their first dance. They held each other so close, as if they were one.

"Robin, how can something so right be so wrong?"

Robin almost stopped dancing. "What do you mean?"

"I mean the timing, the distance, us. I leave you in the morning, carrying with me a heart full of love for the woman I've waited for all my life."

"Honey," Robin said, "this is the beginning for us. I promise you this much, I will make a way to see you every chance I get."

They danced until the restaurant closed. For the remainder of the night, they held each other as they lay in bed. No lovemaking, just holding on to the short time they had to be together. Then it was daybreak, time to go to the airport.

Robin said, "I've packed everything and soon you'll be in sunny warm Florida."

With a sad expression on his face, O.J. said, "Yes, I will be in Florida, but my heart will remain in Westchester. Let's do this. Let's get to the airport."

The ride to the airport seemed endless. Both were very silent.

As they drove, O.J. said, "Once we're at the airport, please just let me out in front. I want you to head back home and be careful driving. You know how I worry about you in this weather. Call me on my cell phone; leave me a message to let me know you made it safely. Promise me you'll do that for me, honey."

"I promise, O.J."

"I hate farewells," he said. "So once you drop me off, let's just kiss, and I'll walk straight until I see you next time. Good-byes are so final. This is the beginning for us, 'cause I'll be sending for you in a few weeks."

They were at the airport. Robin parked the car in front, tears falling from her eyes; she was trying so hard not to be an emotional wreck. O.J. took a hankie from his jacket, wiped the tears, placed it in her hand and said, "I love you with every breath I take, and I promise to see you in a few weeks." He kissed her with all his might. Then he removed his bags from the car and started walking toward the door.

Robin immediately unbuckled her seat belt and ran toward O.J. yelling, "I love you! See you soon!"

"Baby, please don't make this harder than it is. Please go, and drive safely, and don't forget to call."

They departed, both broken-hearted, O.J. on a plane to Florida and Robin on her way home.

Robin called O.J. on his cell phone.

"O.J., I'm missing you already. Let me just say these past few weeks have been wonderful. I never thought I'd meet anyone like you. Thank you for being you. Please call me when you land in Florida. I love you."

Daytona Beach, Florida

O.J. was riding in a daze. The pilot announced they'd be landing in Daytona Beach in 15 minutes. For the first time, O.J. dreaded hearing the name of the place in which he lived. His mind and heart were left in Westchester, New York, where he wanted to be.

O.J. called Robin as soon as he got off the plane.

"Hi, baby. I made it safely. I heard your message, and the feeling is mutual. I'm missing you, too. Robin, listen, if you need to call me, I've given you all accessible numbers to reach me. I'll be sending for you in two weeks, and we'll decide on a date tomorrow. Just wanted to tell you 'I love you and thank you for making my stay lovely'."

"I love you too, O.J. I'm sure the kids are dying to see you. Did you have a good flight?"

"To be honest with you, no, I didn't. I left a part of me there with you. I'm feeling a little sad on the inside," O.J. admitted.

Robin said, "Honey, I understand; so am I, but we'll get through this. Listen, I want you to focus on us being together again soon, not our distance. We'll see each other real soon. I'll call you tomorrow."

"I love you, Robin. Lock up, until tomorrow."

"I love you, too. Later."

O.J. spotted his son waiting to bring him home. He realized at that moment that his son had grown into a young man. He wondered how the kids would react if he left their mom.

His daughter Nichole was running toward him. "Daddy, Daddy!"

O.J. picked Nichole up and gave her a big hug. "I've missed Daddy's favorite girl," he said. "Have you been a good girl?"

Nichole said, "Yes, dad. I'm glad you're home."

The kids were there to greet O.J., but Samone wasn't. O.J. expected no less of her. He was relieved that she didn't come along with the kids.

O.J. asked his son, "Junior, is your uncle A.J. back from L.A?"

"Yes, dad, he was by the house this morning. He says for you to call him when you get in."

O.J. was glad to see his kids, but he also longed for Robin. He and the kids went home, and O.J. called his brother.

"A.J. speaking."

"Hey, bro. I'm home in lovely Daytona Beach."

A.J. said, "What's up, little bro? Aren't you glad to be home?"

"A.J., man, we need to meet at peace ground. I've got some things on my mind I need to talk to you about."

"Call it. Your time is mine."

"How's 10 p.m. tonight? I'll bring some beer?"

A.J. said, "Fine by me. See you then, bro. Peace."

Samone came in from shopping. "Hello, O.J. How was the training?"

"Hi, Samone, everything went well. I passed my certification."

Samone kissed him on the cheek. "We missed you around here. The kids seem so happy you're home now, and things can get back to normal."

O.J. said, "Normal? What do you mean?"

Samone said, "I mean with the kids, and maybe we can work on us too, O.J. I know things haven't been right between us in a while. Your being gone has made me realize a lot. I'm willing to work at it if you are."

This was the last thing O.J. needed to hear. "Samone, please, can we talk about this some other time? I'm really exhausted from the trip."

"Fine, O.J.!" Samone said with an attitude. "Did you at least miss me?"

O.J. said, "Yeah, Samone, I missed you. I'm going to take a nap. We'll talk later."

O.J. was avoiding Samone. He couldn't look her in the eye. Guilt was eating him alive. Samone was a good mother to the kids and a hard-worker, but the love he once felt for her was gone. O.J. couldn't wait to talk to his brother. He was overwhelmed with thoughts of Robin and guilt from Samone. His head began to throb so he lay down until it was time to meet with A.J.

Samone came into the bedroom, undressed and showered. O.J. had his back turned as if he were asleep. Samone lay beside O.J., trying to fumble with his ears to wake him. O.J. knew exactly what she wanted. He had been away for six weeks, and he knew he'd have to face her wanting to be with him sexually. O.J. turned over, told her he had a headache from the flight, and suggested they pick this up some other time. Samone felt slighted; something wasn't right.

"O.J. you've been gone six weeks, and you're brushing me off," she said. "I know you. What's the problem?"

"Samone, listen, I don't feel well. I'm tired. I've been working double shifts. Please let me rest."

"Fine. I'm not going to push myself on you or anything. I'm going to start dinner."

O.J. knew he couldn't keep this charade up; he'd have to face Samone. His guilt was growing by the minute. He got dressed to go out. He needed to hear Robin's voice.

"O.J., where are you going? I thought you weren't feeling well."

"I'm going to the drugstore to pick up something for this headache, and I'm going to see A.J. while I'm out."

Samone gave him a look. "Your brother means more to you than I do."

O.J. sighed. "Samone, please don't start. I've only been back a few hours and already you want to start."

He grabbed his car keys and headed for the door. He didn't want to argue with Samone. He knew that the argument was because of his not paying any attention to her. In his heart, he knew Samone was right; he had been gone six weeks, and any man in love with his woman would want to spend time with her after so many weeks. But

135

his mind was on Robin. He realized how much Robin meant to him. He began to lie to Samone to make room for Robin.

O.J. called Robin.

"Hello?"

"Hi, baby. How you doing?"

He could hear the smile in Robin's voice. "Thinking of you. Missing you, O.J."

"The feeling is mutual."

"How are the kids?" Robin asked. "Were they glad to see you?"

"Yes, they were. They're fine. Thanks for asking."

"Honey, what's wrong? Something sounds different in your voice."

O.J. said, "I'm fine. I think it's the weather change. It's 80 degrees here – from the snow to heat. I'm feeling a little sick. I'm on my way to the drugstore to pick up some cold medicine."

Robin said, "I'm sitting here looking out the window watching the snow fall. Honey, please take care of yourself. I'll worry about you."

"I promise I'll do that for you. Hey Robin, listen, I want to see you soon. Check your schedule for the weekend of the fifth, which is the week after next. I want to send for you. I need to see you. Just missing you, that's all."

"I can do that, O.J. I'm missing you too, and some warm weather would be nice. O.J., are you sure you're all right?"

"Baby, really I'm fine. Just called to say I love you. I need to see you soon."

"Honey, I love you too, and I'll be there," Robin promised.

"Sounds good. My time is running out. I'll call you tomorrow. You lock up and be safe. I care for you, Robin. I'm in love with you. I'll call you tomorrow evening. Have a good night."

"Take care of that cold. Love you."

O.J. felt better just hearing her voice. He sure had a situation on his hands to deal with. He knew he wanted Robin in his life. He was on his way to peace ground to meet A.J. He could express his deepest feelings with his brother. They were very close.

Peace Ground

O.J. arrived before A.J., which was usual. A.J. had never been a punctual person. O.J. popped open a beer and looked out over the city. Daytona was beautiful at night, with the houses all lit up along the beach. Their peace ground building was an old abandoned building A.J. had purchased to renovate as part of his real estate ventures. He had a lot of business ventures and wasn't hurting for money.

A.J. finally arrived. "Hey man, what's up? You looking out over the city like you wanna jump. Things can't be that bad."

O.J. turned to greet his brother and hugged him.

"Man, it's good to see you, A.J. Thanks for watching the family while I was away. So how was L.A?"

A.J. popped a beer. "L.A. was good to me. I closed a deal for a half million. Property I've bid on for a condo complex. Life is good. Hey, you all right, man?"

O.J. came right to the point. "I got a situation on my hands. I met the woman of my dreams. Man, she's everything I ever wanted. I had a wonderful time these past few weeks in Westchester. I love this woman."

"Hey, bro, hold up. That's too strong of a word for my vocabulary. Is she really all that, O.J?"

"She's all that and more," O.J. said. "She makes me feel alive on the inside, man. She's all that."

A.J. shook his head. "Damn, what did this woman do to my brother?"

"Man, she loved me the way a man is supposed to be loved. A. J., you know things are dead with me and Samone."

A.J. said, "I don't see how you tied yourself down all these years, living a lie, settling for less."

"I did it for the kids," O.J. said. "I didn't want to walk out on them like Dad did to us. I wanted my family complete. Even if that meant giving up my happiness."

A.J. had a sad expression on his face. He struggled with his feelings concerning their father. "O.J., man, I respect that. Our dad wasn't a man. I don't acknowledge him as my father. Not the way he did Mom and us. I hate that man. If I saw him in the streets I'd treat him like a stranger."

O.J. knew this was a difficult subject for A.J. O.J. felt that the feelings A.J. harbored for their father had hindered him over the years from getting close to anyone.

Finally A.J. said, "O.J., look you've got a situation that's really not complicated at all."

O.J. frowned. "What do you mean? Haven't you heard a word I said?"

A.J. said, "Yes, I've heard every word, and you're missing the point."

"And what might that be? Talk to me," O.J. demanded.

"Man, it's simple. I do it all the time. You just keep them both. Samone is in Daytona, and Robin is in Westchester. You make ways to visit Robin without Samone finding out and everybody is happy."

"A.J., that's where you miss the point. I love Robin and I can't do her like that. She and Samone both deserve fairness."

A.J. said, "Well, my brother, you've solved your own dilemma. Leave Samone for Robin."

"You and I both know it's not that simple. Look, I need you to do something for me," questioned O.J.

A.J. said, "Name it. Whatever I can do to help my bro."

"I promised Robin I'd send for her in a few weeks. A.J., can you make all the arrangement for me?"

A.J. grinned. "Not a problem. I know all the hideaway spots. Maybe a suite on the beach would be nice. She'd like that. I'll have all the arrangements complete by tomorrow. I'll just call my travel agent. O.J., stop worrying. Haven't I always come through for you?"

"Yes, you have A.J. It's just that I've never been in a situation like this before."

"Man, listen to me; I won't lead you wrong," A.J. said. "I do it all the time, juggle my women. If one don't do then I go to the next."

"Yeah, I know, A. J., but that's not my style. I've been with Samone for over 20 years, and there's nothing left to the relationship. We're just barely civil to each other and that's because of the kids."

"All the more reason to keep Robin on the side," A.J. said.

O.J. shook his head. "A.J., she's better than that. We click. Man, I love her."

A.J. said, "Yeah, I hear you. Have another beer, relax, things will be all right. Samone is a good woman, O.J. I mean, she's done well for my niece and nephew."

O.J. nodded. "I know, A.J.; I can't take that from her. She's a good mother. But, man, we've grown apart. So many times I wanted to leave, but I stayed for the kids."

A.J. patted his brother on the back for being twice the man their father wasn't. "I say it's your time now, bro. God has smiled on you. So reap the benefits and be happy. If Robin makes you happy, enjoy whatever time you have to be with her."

O.J. said, "There's one more thing."

"Put it on me, bro."

"Why am I feeling so guilty? I couldn't even look at Samone."

"My brother, lesson number one in the game is never give yourself away. Act normal, O.J. Women can sniff these things out. Samone is a very intelligent woman. So be cool. You've been gone over a month. Tonight of all nights you should be loving Samone, whether you feel like it or not. Lesson number two: never leave any clues."

"A.J., this isn't a game."

"Like hell it isn't! You've got three players and you're the number one player. If you listen to me you can master this game."

"A.J., you don't understand."

"O.J., I understand more than you know. I may not be in a committed relationship like you and Samone. There are women out there who put their claims on me; each of them thinks they are the one, and I keep them all thinking that way. You know I always had a couple of spares in the trunk. That's where you got to get. It's all about you," A.J. boasted.

"Man, just make the arrangements for me, okay A.J.? I need to head on back to the house."

They hugged and parted to go their separate ways. A.J. felt his brother's uneasiness, and he was worried about him. Before he pulled off in his car, A.J. rolled the window down.

"Listen man, I never told you this, but I'd give anything to be in your shoes. Man, you've done the right things by your kids, and if Robin is who you want, then it's your time to be happy. I'll do all I can to help. Just keep your head straight."

O.J. said, "Thanks, A.J. Just take care of the arrangements for me."

"I got this, man. Go on home and relax. I'll call you tomorrow with the details."

O.J. drove off feeling a little better, knowing that he would see Robin in a few weeks.

At the House

He headed on home to deal with Samone. He pulled up in the driveway and their bedroom light was on. He knew Samone had waited up for him. He sat in the car collecting his thoughts. He thought about what A. J. had said about not giving himself away. He knew he had to make love to Samone to keep her suspicions down. He went into the house. Samone was dressed in her red see-through negligee. O.J. knew exactly what she wanted.

"Are you feeling any better after seeing your brother?" Samone asked.

"Yeah, I just wanted to thank him for looking after you all while I was away."

"How's your headache?"

"I'm feeling better. Maybe the night air helped."

"Come lie with me, O.J."

O.J. knew that was his lead. He lay next to Samone thinking about Robin. He looked at Samone, but only saw Robin. He made love to Samone, but felt Robin. Samone, completely satisfied, fell asleep. O.J., feeling guilty, got up and went to the living room and fell asleep on the couch until the next morning. He awoke to the smell of food cooking in the kitchen.

Samone said, "Good morning, O.J."

"Good morning. The kids still asleep?"

"Yes, they're still sleeping. O.J., about last night...you were great. Maybe you should go away more often."

O.J. couldn't look Samone in the face, knowing it was because he was thinking about Robin.

"I guess I missed you, Samone," he managed to say.

Samone said, "O.J., listen, I know things haven't been what they should be with us, but I'd like to try to make things better. I may get lucky tonight again," she said with a smile. "Breakfast is ready and lunch is in the fridge. I'll be home early tonight."

"Have a good day, Samone."

"You do the same."

145

O.J. couldn't remember the last time Samone got up early to make breakfast before work. He knew then that he must have performed really well. He also knew he couldn't go on fantasizing about Robin while making love to Samone. *I have to tell Samone the truth* he thought. *Or Robin.*

O.J. ate and left for work. While he drove, he listened to his cell phone messages. Robin had left an early message for him before she went to work. O.J. had turned off his cell phone last night, but what if he hadn't and Samone had picked up the phone? He knew he had to find a way to keep the phone out of Samone's sight. O.J. thought he could have all his calls transferred to A.J.'s voice mail. O.J. figured he'd call Robin later and get in touch with A.J. to make sure he didn't have a problem with him transferring the calls.

He called A.J. "Hey, man, come by the house this evening. Have dinner with us. I need another favor."

"I can't. I've got a business engagement tonight, O.J. By the way, all the arrangements are set. I've got Robin booked on a flight on the sixth, returning to Westchester on Monday the ninth. Hotel arrangements are set, too."

"Hey man, thanks. You're the greatest, A.J. I can't wait to call and tell Robin. Now I need your help getting me out of the house that weekend."

"Not a problem. Just leave that up to me. I'll take care of Samone. I'll just tell her I need you to drive me on one of my business ventures."

O.J. said, "Good idea. I'm definitely going to need your help pulling this off."

"O.J., stop worrying. I got your back. Just relax. What else do you need, bro?"

O.J. remembered the reason why he'd called. "Never mind; I think I can take care of the phone."

"What about the phone?"

O.J. said, "Well, I gave Robin my cell number and I didn't want to chance Samone picking it up at night."

A.J. said, "Man, all you do is leave the phone in the car, turn it off, and check all messages from the phone in the house. That way if you have to call Robin back, you go out and make the call."

"You're sly, man. What would I do without you, A.J.?"

A.J. laughed. "Like I told you, be master of the game."

"OK, A.J. Look, thanks, I'll talk at you soon."

O.J. phoned Robin to tell her about the arrangements for her to come to Florida. He got her voice mail. "Hi, this is Robin, I'm unavailable. Please leave a message."

"Hi, baby. Hope you're having a good day. I've got good news. All the arrangements have been made for the trip. I'll call you later with details. I love you. Later."

O.J. was feeling on top of the world, knowing he was going to see Robin soon. He felt that nothing could spoil his day.

Back in Westchester

Robin was on the phone with Ellen. "Robin, girl, how you holding up? I know you miss your man."

"I miss him so much. He's made arrangements for me to fly to Florida. I'm going for sure. I haven't spoken to him yet about the details, but I'm excited about it."

"See, Robin? I told you that you guys would work through the distance. We'll have to go shopping. It's warm in Florida this time of the year. How long you staying for?"

"Maybe just the weekend."

"What matters most is, you get to see each other. Speaking of seeing each other, how about a movie this weekend?" Ellen asked.

"Sounds good. I've got finals coming up soon and work is keeping me busy, too. It will be nice to get out. Take my mind off of things."

Ellen said, "OK, it's a date. I'll give you a call back later. I've got a 3 p.m. with someone T.D.H."

Robin asked. "T.D.H.? What's that?"

Ellen laughed. "Tall, dark and handsome. Robin, not only is he available, but I think he's not only just interested in my work. This is the third meeting he's called with me in less than a week."

"Knock him dead, girl! I'm glad you're taking notice. You've got so much to offer, Ellen. Give me a call later."

"Will do. Talk at you later."

Florida

Samone was at work and on the phone with a travel agent.

"Ms. Henderson," the travel agent said, "I've booked two flights for the sixth of February, and a package at the luxury Sky Hotel. Would you like to reserve this with a credit card?"

Samone said, "Yes. I'm surprising my husband with a weekend getaway. Sort of a second honeymoon in Jamaica."

"We offer the Honeymoon Suite with this package on a special," the travel agent said. "Are you interested?"

Samone said, "Why not? Please reserve that, and I'll pick up the tickets because I want to surprise him."

· "Everything is confirmed, then. Thank you, Ms. Henderson."

O.J. was in for a shock because Samone had planned a getaway trip for the very same weekend he'd planned for himself and Robin. Samone thought the idea of the two of them getting away would enhance their relationship. Samone wanted to tell him the news after he made passionate love to her. She had realized, with O.J. being away, how important it was to save their relationship from dying. She and O.J. had gotten too comfortable with the way things were, and if one of them didn't do something about it, it was going to fade away.

She figured she'd start the evening off by sending the kids to her sisters for the night, since it was Friday. She'd get off work early, fix a nice dinner with all of O.J's favorite food, and they'd have the house to themselves.

They were both in very good moods but for different reasons.

O.J. had ended his workday. He figured he'd stop at a pay phone to call Robin before going home, to give her the details of the trip. "Hi, sweetheart. How was your day?"

"Just grand," Robin said. "It's even better when I heard your message. So tell me, honey, when will I be seeing you?"

"Baby, you've got an early flight, 7 a.m. on February 6th, putting you in Florida at 11:30 a.m. and in my arms as soon as you land."

Robin said, "O.J., thank you. I can't wait to see you. What should I bring? Will I meet the kids? Where will we stay?"

"Baby, slow down," O.J. said. "One question at a time. Bring summer wear; it's warm here. I've arranged a suite for us on the beach. As for the kids, it's a little early in the relationship. I want to tell them about you first. Do you understand?"

Robin said, "Yes, of course I understand, O.J. I'm sorry, I'm just so excited. In less than a week and a half we'll be in each other's arms again."

"Yes, baby, and I can't wait to see you in a swimsuit. In fact, I'll pick one up for you, if that's OK."

"That's fine, O.J. How's your cold? Are you feeling better?"

"I'm fine, Robin, I just can't wait to see you. Listen, baby. I'm on a pay phone 'cause my cell is on a charge. Let me call you tomorrow. You know I love you, don't you?"

Robin said, "Yes, I do, and I love you too, honey. By the way, O.J., thank you."

"The pleasure is all mine. Now you be sure to lock the doors. Sleep tight, my love. Call you tomorrow."

"Love you, O.J. Later."

He. hung the phone up with a smile on his face and went home to unwind from a long workday.

He walked into the house to smell the aroma of collard greens, fried chicken and peach cobbler. What was the occasion? He wondered. Samone came from the kitchen with a glass of wine in her hand.

"Hi, O.J. You're home early. I'm not finished cooking yet."

"Hi, Samone. Where are the kids?"

Samone said, "They're over at my sisters for the night. I've cooked you a nice dinner, rented a few movies. I figured we could enjoy ourselves tonight, just the two of us."

O.J. looked at Samone like he smelled a rat, but he wasn't going to let anything spoil his secret happiness over Robin's visit.

"That's nice, Samone," he said. "I'm going to shower before dinner."

"O.J, would you like a glass of wine or a beer?"

O.J. said, "Nothing, thank you. I'll just take my shower for now."

O.J. knew he couldn't avoid the evening. Samone had gone out of her way to be rid of the kids, and she'd cooked all his favorites. He knew he had to go along with her. O.J. was beginning to feel guilty again, and then he thought about what A.J. had said to him: Master the game, play along.

O.J. couldn't remember the last time he and Samone had had an intimate dinner together. His mind kept returning to Robin. He and Samone were at the dinner table. Samone was so eager to tell him of her plans, her surprise trip.

"O.J., how's the dinner?"

"Dinner is delicious, Samone. You haven't cooked like this in a long time."

Samone said, "I have another surprise for you later. Why don't you relax and put in a movie while I clear the table?"

O.J. went into the living room to put a movie in. Samone came out of the bedroom in a black teddy. O.J. couldn't believe his eyes. Samone had never been so aggressive. He was thinking that she must somehow know about Robin. Samone lured O.J. to the bedroom, and they made love. O.J., thinking about Robin, once again gave an Oscar-winning performance. He rolled over, feeling the guilt. Samone lay in total satisfaction.

Samone smiled. "O.J., that was good. Listen, I have a surprise for you."

O.J., really feeling the guilt, turned around to look at Samone. "What is it?"

"I've planned and paid for a trip for the two of us to Jamaica. Honey, I told you I wanted to try, so I've scheduled a weekend getaway for February the sixth, returning the eighth."

O.J. jumped out of bed in total surprise and anger.

"You did what? And why didn't you check with me first?"

"That's why it's called a surprise, O.J. What seems to be the problem? Why are you getting so loud and overreacting?"

O.J. was trying not to give himself away. "Samone, the thought is nice, but I'm scheduled to work that weekend. You should have checked with me first."

Samone began to cry. "The one time I do something to make this relationship better, and all you think about is work? What about us O.J.?"

Feeling bad about his outburst, O.J. knew that she had gone through a lot of money and heartache to plan the trip. "Samone, the thought is nice and I appreciate it. Stop crying. I didn't mean to upset you. I'm going to take a shower. We'll watch one of those movies you picked up. I'm just surprised about the trip, that's all. Don't worry, we'll go."

O.J. excused himself and went into the bathroom. He was so angry Samone had scheduled the trip for the very same weekend Robin was coming to town. All he could think about was disappointing Robin. His mind raced to A.J. What was he going to do? O.J. knew he had to contact A.J.; this was definitely a peace ground conversation. After he finished with his shower, Samone took hers. O.J. waited until she was in the shower to phone A.J.

The answering machine picked up. "A.J., man, this is very important." I need to talk to you. Call me back at home as soon as you get this message."

Samone went to bed after she took her shower. O.J. stayed in the living room. The phone rang; it was A.J. "O.J., man, what's up? You said it was important."

"Yeah, A.J., man, look, I can't talk now," he said, whispering so as not to wake Samone. "Can you meet me at the Peace ground at 8 a.m. tomorrow morning? It's important."

"Man, what's going on? Are the kids all right, Samone?"

"Yeah, A.J., everybody is fine. It's concerning the matter we talked about the other day. I've got problems."

"OK, brother. I'll be there, and I'll bring the coffee."

O.J. said, "Thanks, man. I'll see you then."

O.J. didn't sleep a wink all night. He lay in the living room on the couch. Samone was knocked out. O.J. was an emotional wreck. What was he going to do? It was breaking day and still no sleep. He went into the kitchen to make coffee. Soon it would be time to meet with A.J. O.J. tiptoed into the bedroom so as not to wake Samone. He wanted to be dressed and gone before she awoke. He figured he'd drive around to clear his thoughts.

While driving, O.J. realized that he didn't want to go away with Samone, but if he backed out of it she'd get suspicious. It would break her heart. After all these years he couldn't believe his going away would make Samone see what was missing in their relationship.

Loretta Heard

Now that he'd met the woman of his dreams, Samone wanted to put forth the effort to try to make the relationship work. O.J. wasn't interested in trying. He was in love with Robin, and he knew he had to be with her.

He took a long drive by the beach. He looked on, watching couples holding hands, taking early morning walks. There was a time when he wanted outings like that with Samone, but neither of them made time for the other. Just a few weeks in Westchester spending time with Robin made up for all the things he and Samone lacked. In just a short period of time Robin had opened up a whole new meaning of life to him. O.J. looked at the clock; it was 7:45 a.m. He headed for peace ground to meet A.J.

Peace Ground

"O.J., man, this better be good," A.J. said. "I don't get up this early on a Saturday for nobody."

158

"Thanks for coming," O.J. said. "You're never gonna believe it. Samone has planned a weekend getaway trip for the very same weekend Robin is scheduled to be here."

"Damn, O.J. you've got to be kidding me."

"I'm serious. What am I gonna do?"

"Cool your brain, my brother. Let me think." A.J. paced back and forth, looking out over the building into the water. "O.J., man, I've got it. I figured it out. I'm brilliant."

"What? Tell me, A.J.," O.J. said with excitement in his voice.

"I'll just pretend I'm you with Robin the whole weekend. We are identical twins, and most people can't tell us apart."

O.J. looked at A.J. with a funny look on his face. "A.J., now I know you've lost it. How do you expect to pull it off? Besides, we may look alike, but we don't act alike. I don't want you getting that close to Robin."

"Excuse me, my brother, you got a better idea?" A.J. interjected. "Don't worry, man. I'll avoid sleeping with her. I'll think of some excuse to avoid the intimacy for a few days."

O.J. was shaking his head. "It won't work, A.J. We'll never be able to pull this off. Man, she's not just any woman I'd pass off to just anyone."

"O.J., I'm your brother. Do I look like just anyone? Tell me, how long is the trip Samone planned?"

"Only for two days," O.J. said. "Leaving on the sixth of February, coming back on the eighth.

A.J. thought about it. "OK, Robin is leaving on Monday, the ninth. That gives you one night to spend with her; then you can perform sexually, making up for lost time. You and I can make the switch just as soon as you get back in town."

"A.J., man, I don't know. I think she'll know the difference. Robin is very intelligent, and she's really into me. I need to think this over."

A.J. said, "It can be done. Remember the tricks we played in high school? No one could tell us apart. Remember those days?"

"Yeah, A.J., I do, but we're not in school anymore. We're grown men now. How are you going to get away with not sleeping with

Robin? The thought of any other man loving her makes my angry, but especially my own twin brother."

"O.J., man, I promise you, I won't lay a finger on her. I'll tell her I'm on medication for a few days, which prohibits me from sexual relations. By then you'll be back in town."

"This is crazy, A.J. Only you would think of such a thing."

A.J. laughed. "Master of the Game, my brother. Master of the Game. It can be done. Samone only knows the difference between us two because she's been around us both all these years. But I'll even bet if we had to pull it off with her we'd get away with it. Looking at you, O.J., is like looking at myself. Sometimes the resemblance frightens even me."

"A.J., I know we look a lot alike, but Robin will know the difference. Trust me; I know. She'll know the difference. It won't work."

"O.J., with the right clothing I could be you. You know how I am with the ladies. No offense to you, but you know I'm smooth."

"That's what worries me, A.J. Let me think this over real hard. Robin is important to me. I'd hate to lose her over the same kind of B.S. we used to pull off when we were kids."

"Look I'm only suggesting an option for you I think can be successfully pulled off. It's all up to you, my brother. You think it over; give me the word and I'll be master of this game. I'll show you, O.J. It can be done. Robin will never know the difference. You're happy, Robin's happy, Samone's happy, and me, I will have done a good deed for my little brother."

O.J. took a good look at his brother and the resemblance was uncanny. They looked just alike. O.J. just shook his head at A.J.

O.J. said, "A.J., man, you're crazy. How can you pose as me?"

"Remember how we used to take turns going to each other's classes, taking each other's exams? We scored then and got away with it. It's no different now. All you have to do is clue me in on things Robin shared with you. Tell me all the things the two of you talked about and things you did. Once I've done my homework, then the game begins."

"Let me think this over. I'll meet you back here tonight around 7 p.m. Remember, A.J., this isn't a game."

"O.J., my brother, don't think too hard. I know how deep in thought you can get. That's why God made us so opposite; I'm the carefree one who takes risks. I'll be here at 7. And, one more piece of advice O.J., get yourself together before Samone catches on."

"Am I that transparent?"

"Yes, you look deep in thought, O.J. Think about the L-word. Remember that?"

O.J. said, "The L-word?"

"Yeah, the L-word...Love which is not in my vocabulary. You said you love this woman, then take a chance on love, O.J. It can be done. If I can entertain Robin for two days, you can have one glorious memorable night with her; then she's back on a plane to Westchester and it's over."

"A.J., I do love her and she's not a pawn to be tossed around. Maybe we can get away with the looks, but how can you occupy her for two days without intimacy? Robin is very affectionate."

"Man, you set the stage before she gets here, O.J. Give her some excuse, like you're being monitored by your doctor for heart blockage. You have to wear heart patches for a few days. You hate the timing of the doctor's testing, but it has to be done on the day she's scheduled to come. You've made all the arrangements and want so desperately to see her, if she can bear with you for a few days. You'll make it all up to her once you remove the patches. You also tell her that if she could sort of help you by not arousing you that would be a lot of undue stress off you. You know, man, who knows?

Once you tell her that, she may change her mind about coming. If she loves you it won't matter if there's intimacy or not. Her concern would be just being with you."

O.J. shook his head. "You're a sick person. Where are we suppose to get heart patches from, and is there even such a test?"

"I don't know if there is, but how would she know if there wasn't? Robin may be intelligent, but she's not a heart specialist. We can use those smoker patches, or get something similar to that without a drug. I have a friend who's a nurse, and with a little charm I can get her to get me something from the hospital like a non-drug patch. Think about it, O.J. I'm brilliant; that's why I'm the number one tycoon real estate broker in the country. I know how to mastermind. It can work. Trust me."

Back in Westchester

Robin's phone rang. "Hello?"

It was Weesee. "Hello, girl, how the hell you doing?"

"Hey, Weesee, I'm fine. How are you doing?"

"Girl, I'm fantastic. You know I struck gold. I'm lying in the sun on the deck of a yacht. Girl, I struck a gold mine, you know? He's not only loaded, but the dick is good, too.

Robin said, "Yeah, Weesee, I heard. Good for you. Thanks for the postcard."

Weesee said, "You're welcome. So, Robin, I hear you got a man. Ellen was telling me he stole your heart."

Robin said, "Yeah, girl, I think this is it."

Weesee said, "Robin, I'm happy for you, girl. Ellen said his last name is O'Neil. He wouldn't happen to be related to that rich real estate guy Aaron O'Neil, would he?"

Robin said, "Weesee, I don't believe so. He never mentioned it to me."

Weesee said, "Girl, that's why I was calling. I figured if he was, you could hook me up. He's worth millions. I met Aaron at a social event last year and, girl, the man is a sight to see. He looks like new money."

Robin said, "Weesee, what about Melvin? I thought you struck gold with him."

Weesee said, "Robin, let me tell you something. You know me. Melvin was my ticket to ride, but now it's time for my ship to come in, if you know what I mean. It's getting old with Melvin. I've spent enough of his money and time. It's time to move on to bigger and better things."

"I think I know what you mean, Weesee. Aren't you ready to settle down and fall in love?"

Weesee laughed. "Yeah, Robin. I can fall real hard on the dollars. Anyway, girl, just wanted to know how you were doing. How's your family? Say hello to everybody, and, Robin, let me know if your man and Aaron O'Neil are related. Maybe we girls can get together real soon. I hear you're going to Florida soon."

Robin said, "Yeah, soon, Weesee. My man is sending for me."

Weesee said, "Now that's what I'm talking about. Make him pay. Listen, girl, gotta run. My massage therapist is here. You take care and keep in touch."

Robin said, "Bye, Weesee. I'll be in touch."

Peace Ground

"A.J. I'm going to think this over real hard. I'll call Robin, sort of set the stage for the patches. If she buys that and sounds just as excited about coming, I'll consider the plan."

"That's what I wanted to hear. Listen, my brother, I've got to run. Got someone keeping my bed warm, and I shouldn't keep her waiting.

167

Let's meet back here at 7 p.m. and I'll bring the liquor, 'cause you look like you need a strong drink."

"Peace, A.J. I'll see you later."

O.J. sat on the roof of the building wondering if he and A.J. could get away with their scheme. He wanted to see Robin so desperately he'd do anything just to spend one night with her. One thing he was sure of, he couldn't get out of his trip with Samone. O.J. was feeling like he'd gotten in too deep, but it wasn't time for him to reveal the truth. He sat there for three hours just looking out over the water, wondering what to do.

Finally he figured he'd better call Robin, explain to her that something came up and maybe they could change their plans for later in the month. He didn't want to disappoint her, so he figured he'd lie to her about the heart testing and leave the decision up to her about coming. He called her on his cell from peace ground.

"Hello?"

"Robin?"

"Hi, baby. What's wrong? I can hear something in your voice. Are you all right?"

O.J. said, "Yes and no. I mean, I've got good news and some bad news."

Robin said, "Honey, what is it? Tell me what's wrong."

O.J. was silent, feeling bad about lying to her. "Robin, remember I told you I wasn't feeling well?"

"Tell me, O.J., are you OK?"

"Honey, I'm OK. There are just a few precautions the doctor wants me to take. He's scheduled me for a heart monitor testing the weekend you're scheduled to come."

Robin said, "Honey, please don't tell me your heart is bad. I've got to be there for you. I've got to make sure you're relaxed. Nothing could stop me, O.J. I love you, and the thought of you going through this alone would make me sick."

"Baby, I know, and I appreciate that. It's just I had a lovely romantic weekend planned for us, and now I won't be able to perform sexually because of the test. The doctor says any sexual encounters would read rapid heartbeats, and that would falsify the test results."

Robin said, "Honey, it's OK. We'll make up for that later; all I care about is being with you, 'cause I love you. I want to go through this with you. I'm still coming."

"Robin, you'd do that for me? Sacrifice your own need for mine?"

"Yes, O.J. I want all of you in one piece, not half of you. Baby, we'll get through this together."

"Baby, that's why I love you. Listen, I only have to wear the patches for two days, and the third day I'm home free. If you can bear with me, I promise you I'll make up for lost time."

Robin said, "O.J., really it's OK. I love you. Please let me be there for you. Honey, do you want me to come before then? Tell me what I can do."

"Baby, you've done enough just loving me. Listen; promise me you won't worry about this. It's just standard procedure, and the doctor is not saying I have a heart problem; he just wants to cover all bases. I can't seem to shake this tightness in my chest, and he wants to run these tests. Baby, please promise me you won't worry."

Robin said, "I promise, O.J. Are you taking care of yourself? I'm not there to do it for you. Promise me that you'll eat and rest regularly."

"I promise and, Robin, please believe that I love you and would never do anything to hurt you."

"O.J., I trust you. Where is this coming from? Is there more I should know?"

"No, honey. It's just that you've had your share of hurt and heartaches. I want you to know that everything I do is because I love you and would never, ever hurt you. Please believe that, Robin, please."

Robin said, "Honey, I believe you. Let's just pray that all is well with you."

"Robin, I'll be fine. How can anything go wrong with you in my life? You've blessed me to feel, and God blessed me with you. I love you."

"I love you too, O.J., and it's settled. Our plans remain the same."

"Yes, they do, and I can't wait to see you, hold you and kiss you."

Robin said, "Mr. O'Neil, there will be none of that until your testing is over. Are we both clear on that?"

"Yes, Ms. Jacobs. I'm still going to pick up that swimsuit. We'll have the last night to make up."

"O.J., relax. We'll be fine; don't you worry about that, now promise me."

"I promise, Robin. You know it's a man thang, and I feel bad about it."

"Honey, look, I know what you're capable of doing. I know exactly what you're made of and how good you make me feel. This is only temporary. We both will survive and get through this together. No more talk of it. You're going to follow the doctor's instructions. Have I made myself clear?"

"Yes, Ms. Jacobs. I love you."

"I love you, too."

"Honey, I'm going to go home, get some rest. I'll call you later."

O.J. hung up the phone, hearing the concern in Robin's voice. He didn't want to worry her, but he wanted so desperately to see her. His mind was made up to follow through with the plan even if he had to

lie to make it happen.

Later at Peace Ground

"A.J., I'm not much of a drinker, but I need a strong one now. Did you bring anything?"

"Yep, right here. So what's the verdict?"

"I've decided to go through with the plan. A.J., man, I called Robin, and she was worried and wouldn't think of changing her mind about coming. A.J., she loves me. How can I abuse that love?"

"O.J., you're not abusing her. You're doing this because you love her. Now get yourself together and let's discuss the plans in detail."

"Fix me up with one of those drinks and maybe it will all sink in better."

"You got it, my brother. Listen, you've got to relax; you can't slip and let Samone catch on or you'll develop real heart problems."

"I know, you're right."

"Do you have any pictures of Robin?" A.J. asked.

O.J. said, "Yes, I do, in my locker at work," O.J. answered.

"Good. Get them to me so I know what she looks like when I meet her at the airport. Now, let's go over every detail from day one until you left Westchester. O.J., I'm recording this; I brought along this mini recorder so I can memorize the details."

"I have one question for you."

A.J. sipped his drink. "Talk to me, my brother."

"How can you detach yourself emotionally from all the women you've encountered A.J.? You've had some beautiful women in your path, and you don't seem to involve yourself for long with any of them."

"Man, it's simple, just like a business deal. Everybody is looking to profit from something. I've attained a successful life for myself. There's no time to settle down. I have to keep it movin'."

"I know your success has earned you much financially, but what do you do when loneliness sets in? Do you ever think about kids and a wife?"

"Now you're getting deep on me, O.J. If kids were in the plan that would be great, but I have my nieces and nephews. As for a wife, I wouldn't want to settle down with all the traveling I do. I'm on the go too much to limit myself or anyone else. I don't have time to get lonely, and everywhere I go I know and meet people. There are just too many beautiful women in this big world for me to just pick one."

"Sometimes I admire your life style, and as your brother I'm often mistaken for you, which earns me privileges, but other times I worry about you A.J."

"You worry about me? Why?"

"A.J., I know you've never gotten over what Dad did to us, and I know family life is something you run from because you're afraid of losing."

"So you think you got me all figured out, Dr. Psychology? You're far from the truth, O.J. I spent three lovely days with our sister Diane and she had the same assumption. Why are the two of you on my case so much? I like my life."

"A.J., maybe it's because Diane and I both love you. How are Diane and the kids?"

"They're fine," A.J. said. "I love the two of you as well, but this is my life, OK? I've done my share of spoiling our sister. I can't resist her whenever she needs something. She looks at me with those light brown eyes of hers and I see Momma all in her. O.J., she turned out to be a fine woman."

"She does look a lot like Mom. I appreciate you looking after both Diane and me. Mom would be so proud of you."

"OK, O.J., let's get back to the plan. Tell me about how and when you met Robin."

O.J. began to talk about his relationship with Robin as if it had happened just yesterday. A.J. was recording every word.

Finally O.J. said, "That's everything, A.J. That's the story of our romance. I love her so much."

"She sounds like a special lady. I noticed how your face lights up just giving me the details. Are you going to eventually tell her the truth?"

"Yes. I will even if it means losing her. She's had her share of headaches, and I hate to add to the list. One thing I'm sure of and that's my love for her. She gives a new meaning to my life."

"O.J., man, that's deep. I didn't realize things were that bad with you and Samone."

"We're only together for the kids. Before my trip to Westchester, there were months without any intimacy. We were like roommates and business partners. We both went our own ways unless it involved activities with the kids. I had forgotten what it was like to have that closeness with a woman. We lost that long ago."

A.J. shook his head, "Man, the two of you grew up together as sweethearts and now the flavor is gone after all those years. Well, I can say that she's a good mother to my niece and nephew. I'll give her that. O.J., whatever you decide to do, I'm in your corner and you know I got your back."

O.J. said, "Thanks, man. How about a refresher on the drink?"

"You got it, brother. Listen, I have to prepare Samone for the trip you'll be taking with me the day you all get back. I'll set the stage for that so she doesn't suspect anything, and that will give you all night with Robin. I'll stop by the house tomorrow and drop a few hints so she'll know."

"I can't thank you enough, A.J. You know I'd do the same for you if I could." They toasted each other with their drinks.

"I know, my brother, 'cause we're blood. Look, I'm leaving for Chicago day after tomorrow, so I'll stop by the house tomorrow evening. We'll get this thing started."

O.J. said, "Sounds good, and I'll give you Robin's picture then. When you get her from the airport, let her freshen up, then take her around sightseeing or something."

"O.J., stop worrying; leave that up to me. You're talking to Mr. Entertainment, remember?"

"Please don't overdo it. I mean, you're used to high class places, A.J. and she knows I don't have it going on like that to afford such places. Just keep it kinda low-key."

"Let me handle this. I know exactly what's affordable to you. I'll show her a good time. Don't worry about that. I'll play the role. Who knows you any better than I do?"

"OK. I'm leaving it all in your hands, A.J."

"She'll be in good hands. I won't let either of you down. Listen, man, I got to get movin'. I've got something lined up for tonight. Are you relaxed about this?"

"Yes, let's do it."

A.J. said, "Deal; then you keep it straight on the home front. I'll be over there tomorrow night. Keep your head together, O.J., and you'll see the love of your life soon."

O.J. hugged his brother before parting. Feeling buzzed from the drink, he was also feeling comfortable about his decision. He sat at peace ground for hours contemplating what could go wrong in the switch. He convinced himself that if he and A.J. got away with it in school without anyone catching on, why couldn't they get away with it now? It was settled in his mind.

Back in Westchester

Ellen called. "Robin, I have a date with Mr. T.D.H. His name is Dameon. I'm so excited."

"That's terrific! You've got to look sexy. Wear something tight and slinky to show off that big butt of yours."

"I don't know," Ellen said. "It's sort of like a business dinner to go over contracts. We've been spending a lot of time together. He's definitely single and available. You should see how the women flock around him. Like bees on honey."

"Girl, he sounds like he's got it going on. Ellen, you deserve that. What can I do to help you prepare?"

Ellen said, "Funny you should ask. I need to borrow your pearl necklace."

Robin said, "Fine; stop by after work. Bring your outfit along so I can give you my opinion."

"OK, Robin. He's tall, dark like chocolate and he's very smart."

Robin said, "You're very intelligent too, Ellen, so he's got himself a prize. Oh, I meant to tell you, Weesee called the other day."

"How's she doing?"

Robin laughed, "You know Weesee; crazy as ever. She was asking me if O.J. was any relation to some rich real estate tycoon named Aaron. You know Weesee, always sniffing out new prospects with money."

Ellen asked, "Is there any relation? Is O.J. loaded, too?"

Robin said, "I really don't believe so. O.J. never said anything to me about a brother named Aaron. He mentioned his sister Diane. I haven't asked, 'cause of the plans for the trip and now his health."

"His health? Is something wrong?" Ellen asked.

"I'm praying there isn't. As a precaution, the doctor is monitoring his heart the weekend I'm scheduled to see him. Ellen, I'm worried about him."

"Girl, I know you got to be and knowing you, wild horses wouldn't keep you from him now."

Robin said, "You're right. I got to see him, be with him, and make sure all is well. Hopefully the test will be good."

"Girl, it's always something. Listen, I've got another call coming in; I'll stop by after work. Try not to worry, Robin. I know you."

"OK, Ellen, see you later."

She had barely hung up the phone when it rang again. It was Raine. "Hey, Robin, what's up?"

"Raine, how you doing? It's so good to hear from you. How are the boys?"

"I'm fine, everybody is good. Just had you on my mind. I get homesick sometimes. Atlanta has been a big adjustment for me."

"Raine, it's all new to you. Once you learn your way around you'll be OK," Robin tried to comfort her.

"Yeah, I guess you're right. How's Ellen? I spoke to Weesee last week with her crazy self. As always, she had me dying laughing, in stitches."

Robin said, "Ellen is good. She's successful with her new job, and she met someone. I know I spoke with Weesee a few days ago, too. She sounds good," Robin replied.

Raine said, "Yeah, Weesee was telling me you met someone in Florida. Is he nice, Robin? Are you happy?"

"Yes, to both questions. Raine, he's perfect for me. You'd like him. I'm going to Florida next week. When I get back I'm going to plan a big dinner party and I want you to come. I'll invite you, Weesee, Ellen and my family; then everybody can meet my man. Will you come, Raine?"

"Robin, I wouldn't miss it for the world. You're my girl. Just let me know in advance so I can make arrangements for the boys. I hate to take them out of school."

"Don't you dare think of leaving my godsons. I'll make it on a weekend so that way you can bring them along. I'd love to see them; I bet they've grown. If money is tight, I'll pay for the boys."

"It's a deal, Robin. I'd love to see everybody. You sound very happy, and I hope this guy is right, 'cause you deserve someone to love."

"Thanks, Raine. I think he's the one."

"Well, we will all get to meet him one day. Listen, you enjoy Florida and be safe. Send us a postcard."

"I'll do that. Give my boys a kiss and tell them I love them and will see them soon."

"Take care." Raine hung up.

Back in Florida

Samone opened the door. "Hi, A.J. Come in. O.J. is in the family room watching basketball."

A.J. said, "Samone, I hear you guys are going to Jamaica for a few days?"

"Yeah. You know your brother and I work so much we hardly have time for each other. I thought a mini vacation would do us both some good."

A.J. said, "That was thoughtful of you. I came by to ask a favor of my brother if it's no bother to you. The day you all get back, I'm going to need O.J. to travel with me and drive my spare car to Atlanta. I'm auctioning off both cars, and we'll fly back the next day. Do you think that'll be a problem, Samone?"

Samone said, "Not a problem for me, A.J. I'm not driving. Talk that over with your brother."

A.J. knew Samone's answer that she didn't care that would excuse O.J. for the night to be with Robin.

"Let me go in there and distract him from his game. Where are the kids, Samone? I've got something for them."

Samone said, "Junior is in his room. Nichole is at her piano lesson. A.J., you have got to stop spoiling these kids. Have some children of your own."

A.J. never did like Samone's sarcastic attitude. She always said what was on her mind. He excused himself and went to the family room.

"Hey, man, it's a go. I dropped the seed for you being with me. I told Samone you'd be driving my spare car to Atlanta with me to an auction. So it's set. She didn't have a problem with it."

"That sounds good. Hey A.J., by the way, how do you come up with all these ideas?"

"Easy," A.J. said, "mind over matter. Did you bring the picture?"

"Yes, it's in the car. I'll walk you out when you leave and give it to you."

"OK, listen, on our way out, mention the drive to Atlanta so Samone will let it sink in."

O.J. said, "Got it."

A.J. said, "OK, let's make moves. I did what I had to do; now I got to get movin'."

The two brothers walked through the kitchen where Samone was washing the dishes.

"A.J., how long of a drive is it? We'll fly back?"

A.J. said, "It's not that long. We'll sleep over and get an afternoon flight out the next day."

Samone was taking in every word. O.J. and A.J. went outside to get the picture from the car. A.J. was grinning. "Man, she bought it. You're in there now. We'll make the switch just as soon as you get back. All you have to do is page me. Put 911 in, and I'll meet you at my place. I'll tell Robin it's work paging me; I'll have to leave her for a short time and I'll be right back. Then you'll come back instead. We'll switch clothes. She'll never know."

"A.J., you certainly don't mind taking risks. I hope this doesn't backfire on me. The picture is inside this envelope. Look at it when you leave and call me later."

"Will do, and O.J., keep it straight. Stop worrying. Things will fly. I'll call you later."

Back in Westchester

Ellen's Date

"Ellen, you look very lovely tonight."

"Thank you, Dameon."

"Why don't we start with a cocktail before we get down to business?" He ordered his preference of drink for them both. Ellen didn't like the thought of him not allowing her to order what she liked to drink for herself. After dinner, Dameon and Ellen discussed contracts.

"Ellen, for the fall casual wear line, I'd like to incorporate a six-month agreement. The styles for fall will be very marketable in France. Have you seen the designer sweaters?"

"No, Dameon, I haven't seen the new line, but I propose we extend the contract for a year. Give the sales a chance to fly, make our profits, and then expand if needed."

"That's all well and good, Ellen, but six months is ample enough time." He reached for her hand. "You must see the sweaters. After our deal is closed with Mr. Sinclair – whom I may add, will be meeting us at 8 p.m. to sign the deal -- I'd like to bring you to my place and present to you our new fall sweater line. Do you have any remarks?"

"No, nothing at all, Dameon. Six months it is."

"Good! Now I want you to excuse yourself and freshen up your makeup before Mr. Sinclair arrives. We want to make a lasting impression. This is a million-dollar contract and, believe me, if we land it, you'll be compensated personally by me. Now run along and make yourself pretty."

Ellen excused herself. She didn't know if she liked his arrogance or not, but he was so cute. She couldn't believe he was taking her to his house after the first date. Was she reading too much into it?

Later, over dinner, Mr. Sinclair said, "Dameon, I must say that I'm very impressed with what you and Ellen have put together here. I'll be happy to sign off on your proposal."

The deal was sealed, and they all shook hands. Ellen had just landed her first million-dollar contract. She was excited. She couldn't wait to give Robin the news.

After Sinclair left, Dameon said, "Ellen, I'd say this calls for champagne, which I just happen to have chilling on ice at my place. Shall we --?"

"Yes, we shall."

Ellen was feeling on top of the world, thinking to herself that Dameon must have had a celebration planned. Certainly he was interested in her, and she couldn't refuse his offer. Besides, a celebration was in order.

They arrived at Dameon's place. His house was huge; more like a mansion. The foyer alone was as big as Ellen's whole apartment. He welcomed her into the living room while he went to get the champagne. Ellen was very impressed with the décor. Dameon was very immaculate and had an artistic flair.

"Ellen, would you care for something to eat? The maid has left for the evening, but I'm sure I can prepare a snack."

"No, thank you Dameon. Champagne is just fine."

She was in awe at the house and couldn't believe her eyes. He was definitely Weesee's type. Dameon poured their drinks, and they toasted each other.

"Here's to a job well done, Ellen. I couldn't have done it without you."

Ellen was blushing. "Thank you, Dameon."

"Let me bring you upstairs, Ellen, and show you the fall casual line."

Ellen followed him upstairs. She couldn't believe the size and number of rooms. The room they went into was nothing but a huge walk-in closet with all kinds of women's clothing, designer name clothes from sweaters to coats, all nicely arranged. Ellen couldn't believe Dameon collected every single line he had ever contracted. She was speechless.

"Ellen, what size are you? I'd like to have a sweater designed especially for you."

191

"Dameon, that won't be necessary. But I appreciate the offer. Everything is so expensive."

"I won't take no for an answer." He selected a beautiful cashmere sweater from one of the racks. "I believe this will fit you. I'd like for you to try it on. Make yourself comfortable in the dressing room, and I'll bring it in."

Ellen made her way into the dressing room, a room with mirrors all around and lights around every mirror. She had never seen anything like it. There was a door inside the room; she was curious to know what was beyond the door. She reached for the doorknob, but it was locked. Oh well, she didn't want to be nosy and ask.

Dameon knocked on the door to give her the sweater. It was beautiful. Nothing she owned was that costly. The tag read $850, just for one sweater. Ellen was thinking her entire wardrobe wouldn't add up to that much. She put the sweater on, and it fit like her skin. What a difference money can buy. Dameon was waiting outside the room for her.

"You look so elegant, Ellen. It fits you perfectly. It's yours, and it's my pleasure. I'll have another made for you."

"Thank you, Dameon," Ellen beamed.

"Now get dressed and let me bring you home. We both have an early morning. I'll give you a garment bag for your sweater. I'll be in the foyer downstairs waiting for you."

Ellen appreciated the sweater, but she felt Dameon was too forward for her. She was attracted to him, but he was very arrogant. She removed the sweater, got dressed and went down to the foyer. Dameon was waiting with a bottle of champagne to give to Ellen to take with her. They went out a different door of the house which led to the garage. He drove his sports car to take her home. Ellen wasn't sure if he was trying to show off or impress her, but impressed she was. He was a gentleman; he opened the car door for her and took her home safely.

Outside her apartment, Ellen said, "Dameon, I had a wonderful evening. Thank you so much for the sweater. Your house was very welcoming and nice."

"Thank you, Ellen, for a job well done. Let me escort you to your door." He walked her to the door, and said, "Good night. See you in the morning."

"Good night, Dameon."

She'd had a nice evening and had made a huge commission, but she was slightly disappointed that he didn't make a pass, or at least kiss her good night.

Meanwhile Dameon, excited about the deal he just closed, wanted to share his news with his close friend and love, Aaron John O'Neil.

He called and got A.J.'s answering machine.

"A.J. It's Dameon. Just called to say my million-dollar account is signed, sealed and will be delivered to the bank tomorrow. Listen, I'd say a celebration is in order. Check your calendar; see if you can meet me in Seattle next Tuesday. I'd love to see you. Call me when you get this message."

Florida

A.J. had arrived home after visiting with his brother. He hung up his coat and out fell the envelope with Robin's picture. With all the business deals on his mind, he had forgotten it. He hung up his coat and opened the envelope. A.J. thought Robin was attractive; she had a beautiful smile. She was very plain compared to all the beautiful models who had crossed his path. Still, he thought Robin was perfect for his brother. He studied the picture carefully, placed it on his night stand so that once he awakened, Robin would be the first face he saw. He was going to study the tape of all the details O.J. had given him, but he wanted to listen to his phone messages first. He was happy to hear Dameon's voice. He returned his call.

Westchester

"Dameon speaking."

"Congratulations, Dameon. I knew you could do it. I had confidence in you all along."

"Thank you, A.J. I need to see you. I'm missing you. Can you make the Seattle trip? Of course I'll spring for the trip. We'll stay at our favorite spot."

A.J. said, "I'll have to check my calendar. That would be relaxing. I've got a lot on my plate, and a few days of relaxation would be nice. I'll get back to you tomorrow. Is that all right?

Hey…..by the way, what are you wearing, Dameon?"

"A hot deep-purple number. Your favorite color. If you make the

Seattle trip, I'll come full of surprises," Dameon coaxed.

"That sounds very enticing. I'll call you tomorrow night.

Congratulations again, Dameon. Talk to you soon."

A.J. had a serious thing for Dameon. They had been off and on in

their relationship for five years. No one else knew of A.J.'s desires

for men, and he kept that a secret especially from his family. Dameon

understood him, the rush he got from business, the pressures of

keeping his image intact. Dameon was his close friend and lover.

They'd often meet in secret places like Seattle, or Paris, whenever

Dameon had business in France.

A.J. had desires for women, too, but what he shared with Daemon

could not compare. A.J. would get attitudes when his brother O.J. and

sister Diane would talk to him about marriage and children. He had a

bisexual lifestyle which he enjoyed. Neither kids nor a wife fit into

that lifestyle. Dameon had a way of easing his tired soul, making him feel very relaxed. A.J. fell asleep listening to his brother's voice on the tape, detailing his relationship with Robin.

Westchester

"Ellen, you never called last night. How did the date go with Dameon?" Robin asked inquisitively.

"We closed the deal! I made a lot of money last night. I also went to Dameon's house, which by the way, is a mansion."

Robin said, "No wonder I didn't hear from you. You went to his house? Do tell!"

"Robin, it's not what you're thinking. We went there to have a glass of champagne to celebrate the deal. He didn't make one pass at me, but he did give me a sweater worth $850."

"Did you say $850 for one sweater? You've got to be kidding."

"Robin, I kid you not. He was very generous. I don't mean to sound so ungrateful, 'cause I've never owned any item of clothing worth that much, and he was the perfect gentleman. When he invited me over, I guess I was expecting a come-on. He's so attractive."

197

Robin said, "Girl, give it time. He'll come around. Just be yourself. So, his house is nice?"

Ellen said, "Robin it's like a celebrity's house. He has a maid, and let me tell you about the dressing room. His dressing room is a walk-in room full of designer clothing. There are mirrors all over the room. I've never seen anything like it in my life."

"Are you serious, Ellen? Those must be all the lines of clothing he's sold."

"Yes, they are. Girl, expensive clothes, too. There was a door inside the room, but it was locked. I'm curious to know what was behind that door."

Robin laughed. "Well, if you hang in there long enough I'm sure you'll find out. Did he ask you out again?"

"No, not officially, that is."

Robin said, "What do you mean?"

"It's always business with him. We're meeting today for lunch. We're working on a new project."

"He keeps coming back to you, Ellen, so that's got to mean something. Give it some time; he'll come around. He's cute, hmmmm?"

"Very. Girl, I've got to have this man. I'm crazy over him," Ellen confided.

"You watch, he'll make a move when you least expect it. You just throw your bait out so he can bite. Be patient, my friend; things will work out."

"Maybe you're right. Thanks, Robin. I'm always giving you advice; it's good to hear my own words."

"That's what friends are for."

"You started packing yet Robin?"

"Yes. I'll be seeing my man in a few days. I'm soooo excited."

"Don't forget the tanning lotion."

Robin laughed. "That was the first thing I bought. Ellen, I got another call coming in; buzz me later."

"Will do. Talk at you later."

Florida

"O.J., you got to meet me at peace ground to go over the details. I'm leaving for Seattle on business on Tuesday. I'll be gone a few days, arriving back before you leave for Jamaica."

"OK, A.J., I'll come straight there after work. Let's make it 6 p.m. Is that good for you?"

"I'll be there. Why don't we get a bite to eat after we talk? Like old times."

"I'd like that. See you soon."

A.J. phoned Dameon's private number. The answering machine picked up: "This is Dameon Davenport; I'm either away on business or engaged in something important. Please leave a message."

A.J. said, "Dameon, hi, A.J. Listen, I've freed my calendar for Seattle. I'll meet you at our spot on Tuesday evening 7 p.m. Dameon, bring all those surprises you've got me fantasizing about. See you soon, my love."

Peace Ground

"What's in the bag?" O.J. asked.

"I went shopping and picked up a few clothes I thought you'd wear, so I brought them along for you to look at."

O.J. looked at what A.J. had bought. "This is definitely my style. I guess you're right; no one knows me like you. I can't remember the last time you wore a pair of jeans."

"Yeah, you're right; it's been a while. It will be nice to dress down for a few days. You know suits are my style. To play the part I have to dress the part."

"Good thinking, A.J. You've got everything under control. I guess that's why you're so good at what you do. You're on top of it all."

"Yes, I've got to be. OK, let's go over everything in detail."

"OK, I'm to page you once I bring Samone home from our trip. Then I'll meet you at your place, change into the clothing you had on, and then go back to the hotel to meet Robin."

"Correct. Remember to put 911 into the page so that I'll know it's you. I've also got some fake patches which you are to place on your chest. Once you're back at the hotel with Robin, after a few hours you tell her your 48 hours of testing is over; then you're home free to do your thang."

O.J. smiled. "It sounds like it could work."

"It's gonna work, my brother. Remember, master of the game. I have a keen memory. I've memorized everything you told me. Just ask a question."

"OK, how did I meet Robin and where was our first date?"

"You were dispatched to her house on a job, and the first date was at the Crown Royal, where the two of you danced until sunset," A.J. finished, throwing in a little humor.

"Good, A.J., you did your homework. I think we can do this."

A.J. said, "Consider it complete. We'll go over the plan one last time when I get back from Seattle. Now let's go eat."

"A.J., thanks. Why don't you let me treat you to dinner? I appreciate all that you're doing for me."

"OK my, brother. You know I've got an expensive appetite."

"OK, I'll dig deep in my pockets. I may have to get a loan, though," O.J. laughed.

They both laughed and then went to dinner.

.

Westchester

Dameon called Ellen. "I'm leaving for Seattle for a few days. I'll need for you to cover the McDonald account while I'm away. Please come by the house around 7 p.m. and we'll go over the details."

Ellen said, "Seven it is, Dameon."

Robin's phone rang. It was Larry. "Hi, Mom, how you doing?"

"I'm fine, son. How's the new apartment? Have you been eating OK?"

"Mom, I'm just fine. I'm not a baby anymore. So, you leave for Florida soon. Are you excited?"

"Yes, baby. I'm long overdue for a vacation." Larry could sense her smiling as she spoke.

"Mom I need to meet this O.J. guy, and he better treat you right while you're there. You've got all the phone numbers to call if things aren't right, don't you?"

Robin laughed. "Yes, I do, son. Anything else?"

"No, Mom, except have a great time and be safe. I love you. You're my Mom and I want you to be careful, OK?"

"Yes, dear. I love you too, and I'll call you before I leave. You need any money or anything?"

"Mom, I'm fine. Gotta get ready for work. Love you Mom; talk at you soon."

"Love you, too, son. Be good."

Robin hung up the phone, smiling over her son's protectiveness. She realized that Larry was growing up, feeling like he was the man in her life.

Dameon's Place

"Please come in, Ellen and make yourself comfortable in the den."

"Thank you, Dameon."

"I've made some tea; please excuse me while I fix it."

Dameon went off to the kitchen. Ellen took work out of her briefcase and reviewed the McDonald account. She heard the phone ring.

"Ellen, help yourself to some tea. I just received an urgent phone call. Would you excuse me for about an hour? I have an important errand to run that can't wait. I'll return as soon as possible. Help yourself to the kitchen, and the rest-room is off the foyer down to your left. I'll make it quick so we can get down to business."

"Not a problem, Dameon. I have enough with the McDonald account to keep me occupied," Ellen reassured him.

"Fine. Make yourself comfortable, I'll return soon."

Dameon went out the front door, leaving Ellen alone in the huge mansion. Ellen felt a little frightened at first. She began to look over the accounts. When she became restless, she put the work aside to find her way to the rest-room. While she was walking down the foyer, she thought of the closed door off the dressing room she had seen on her last visit. Ellen thought this would be the perfect time to see what was behind the door while Dameon was away. She looked out the window to make sure he wasn't home yet, and made her way up the stairs.

There were so many rooms at the top of the stairs, she had to remember which room was the dressing room. The first door she opened was a bedroom, so was the second door. Finally she tried one more door before giving up. It was the dressing room with the secret doorway. She went inside and turned on the lights. She saw the secret door. Hoping it would not be locked, she reached for the doorknob, and it opened! The door opened to a second walk-in closet.

On the inside was a shelf full of wigs on dummy heads, perfectly arranged from blonde to brunette, in different styles as well as lengths. On one side of the wall were huge posters of the most beautiful woman Ellen had ever laid eyes on. The woman looked a lot like Dameon. Could this be Dameon's sister? Or maybe his mom in her younger days? She was trying to figure out what all the wigs were for and for whom when she heard a car pull in the driveway. She hurried out of the room, turned off the lights, shut the doors and quickly made her way back down to the den. She ran as if she were in a marathon race, took her seat, breathless and panting. She took a sip of tea to compose herself.

Dameon strolled in. "Ellen, thank you for waiting. Did you make yourself comfortable?"

Ellen, catching her breath, said, "Yes, very, Dameon."

Dameon settled in a chair across from her. "Well then, let's go over the documents."

Ellen's mind was distracted by what she had seen in that room. She needed to find out if Dameon had once sold a line of wigs and possibly collected them as he did his clothing lines. Maybe Dameon lived with a woman, and no one knew of his secret affair; maybe those things were his mom's or his sister's. Ellen's mind was working overtime. She was so attracted to Dameon, she needed to know who the other woman was in his life.

"Ellen, are you OK? You seem a bit preoccupied. I just asked you the same question twice."

"I'm OK, Dameon. It's been a long day."

"I understand; we'll be wrapping this up soon. Let's go over the figures once more, and then we'll call it a night."

"Sounds good; I'm a bit tired."

"Ellen, you've outdone yourself once again. Everything looks excellent. I'm confident that while I'm in Seattle you'll represent me very well. I'd like to make you a gift of a bottle of very rare red wine from my cellar."

"Thank you, Dameon; that's very kind and thoughtful of you."

Dameon went to the wine cellar. Ellen's mind was in a frenzy trying to figure out who this mystery woman could be. No one she knew had ever seen Dameon out in public with a woman. He always attended social functions alone. In the society papers he was known to be the most available bachelor. All the women flocked around him like flies. Ellen knew she had her detective work cut out for her.

Dameon came back from the wine cellar and offered Ellen the bottle of wine. "This should relax you," he said, "1976 was a good year. Go home, take a nice bubble bath, and tomorrow I'll schedule you for a full body massage with my therapist, my treat."

"Thank you. Dameon; you're so generous."

Dameon returned her smile. "You're welcome, Ellen. I'm only generous to those I care about."

Ellen tried not to show emotion or read too much into those words. "Well, I better go take that bubble bath."

"Let me escort you to your car."

Dameon walked Ellen to her car, and they said their good nights.

Florida: One Week Later

Samone said, "O.J., thank you so much. I was so worried about the trip. You didn't seem too excited about it at first."

O.J. looked puzzled. "What are you thanking me for, Samone?"

"Silly me, I've ruined the surprise. The bikini you bought for me. I'm sorry, but I had to try it on. It's a perfect fit. She threw her arms around O.J. and hugged him.

O.J. had a sour look on his face. "That was a surprise, Samone. You weren't supposed to see it."

He'd been preoccupied with the plans, worried about something going wrong, and forgot to put away the swimsuit he purchased for Robin. Samone had found it and thought it was for her. Tomorrow morning they would leave for Jamaica, and Robin would be in Florida. He hadn't heard from A.J., and he was nervous.

"Samone, has A.J. called?"

Samone said, "Oh yeah, I forgot to tell you; he said his flight was delayed in Seattle. He said he'd call just as soon as he made it in."

"I just wanted him to watch the house while we're away, check on the kids, that sort of stuff," O.J. said.

"Honey, we'll only be gone for two days."

O.J. thought *Honey*? He looked at Samone, wondering what in the hell had gotten into her. "I forgot to pick up shaving lotion," he said, going for his car keys, "do you need anything while I'm out?"

"No, thank you, O.J. Don't be too long. I'd like to close the suitcases."

O.J. had to go out to call Robin one last time and make sure all was well with her. He was worried about A.J. hooking up with him one last time.

Robin answered right away. "Hello?"

"Hi, baby, you all packed?"

"Packed and ready to fly. O.J., I can't wait to see you. My stomach is in knots. I guess it's the anticipation."

"I know, sweetheart. I'm feeling the same way. Especially about depriving you intimately."

Robin said, "Honey, please stop worrying. As long as I'm with you, that's all I care about. You know what time the flight arrives?"

"Yes, I'll be there on time. Robin, I love you."

"I love you, too, O.J. Until tomorrow, my love. Sleep tight. Get some rest."

"Until tomorrow, love. Good night."

"Good night."

O.J. hung up the phone feeling as if the pit of his stomach was falling out. His hands were sweaty, and he felt sick. Where was A.J.? He was getting more anxious by the minute. He tried to contact him. on his cell phone with no luck.

Westchester

"Robin, you've got to wake up. Please pick up. It's important. Thinking about it all is driving me crazy," Ellen complained.

Robin, waking from a sound sleep, said, "Hello, what's wrong? Ellen, are you all right?"

"Robin, are you wide awake? I'm sorry. I know you have an early flight."

"Girl, it's all right. What's going on?"

Ellen sounded hysterical. "Robin, I went into Dameon's secret room a few days ago. I snuck in and there was a shelf full of women's wigs, and on the wall was this huge poster of this beautiful model. Do you think she's his woman? Why would all the wigs be there and locked behind that door?"

"Ellen, calm down. Don't let your imagination get the best of you. Number one, if there was another woman, would he bring you home with him twice? Number two, maybe the wigs are a line of products he sold before he met you. Don't do this to yourself."

Ellen said, "What should I do? Maybe hire a private detective to find out who this mystery woman is?"

"Don't waste your money on an investigator. Trust me; you're getting uptight about nothing. The man is an entrepreneur and a fashion expert. Why wouldn't he have different lines of products, including wigs?"

"Robin, maybe you're right, I'm sorry for disturbing you. It's just been bugging me these last few days, and I wanted your take on it before you left me for Florida. I'm obsessed with it."

"Girl, don't be sorry. I'm your friend. Ellen, give it some time. I don't want you worrying yourself over nothing. Besides, you're in there with him. You've been to his home twice."

"I guess you're right. I apologize for waking you. Listen, you have a good time in Florida. Send me a postcard."

"I'll do better than that. I'll call you as soon as I get there. I want to make sure you're OK, and please try not to worry. Promise me you won't go doing any detective work."

"OK, Robin, I promise. Now go back to sleep. Talk at you soon."

Ellen had been restless since snooping at Dameon's. Dameon was embedded in her mind. She went to the kitchen to pour a glass of the wine Dameon had given her. The phone rang; she thought it was Robin calling her back. "Hello?"

"Ellen, I'm sorry to disturb you so late." It was Dameon.

"Oh, Dameon, it's never too late for you. Is everything all right?" Ellen asked.

"No, as a matter of fact, it isn't. I was calling to ask a favor. I'm stranded in Chicago, and my luggage got put on a different flight. No one else is free to retrieve it for me. Would it be a problem if I asked you to pick up my luggage at the airport tomorrow?"

"Not a problem at all, Dameon. How terrible. How was Seattle?"

"Breathtaking. It was a pleasurable trip. Ellen, you're a dear; thank you so very much. The flight with my luggage will be arriving at 10 a.m. I'll give you the airline and flight number. If you would take my bags to your place, I will pick them up as soon as I arrive."

"It's my pleasure, Dameon. You've been so generous. It's not a problem at all."

"Thanks. And by the way, how have you been sleeping the past few nights, Ellen? I've found that wine is a great relaxer."

"I'm pouring a glass as we speak. I've been sleeping much better, thank you."

"Again, I appreciate your helping me out, and I apologize for the late call. I'll see you the day after tomorrow, Ellen. Good night."

Ellen hung up the phone, shivering pleasantly at the sound of Dameon's voice. She couldn't believe he had called her long distance. She poured a glass of wine to relax her nerves, then another and another. Before she realized it, she had drunk half the bottle. What was this man doing to her? She wondered. Feeling buzzed from the wine and fell asleep on the living room sofa. She was a wreck.

Florida 1 a.m.

O.J.'s phone was ringing. He ran for it so as not to wake Samone. "Hello?"

"What's going on, my brother?"

"A.J., where the hell are you? I've been pacing the floor, worried out of my mind!"

"I'm in your driveway in my limo."

"Limo? I'm getting dressed. I'll be out there in a few seconds," O.J. said angrily.

He opened the door to the limo and noticed his brother in a state of intoxication. A. J. was sloppy drunk. There was an empty cognac bottle on the floor.

"A.J., man, what's going on? You drank that whole bottle of cognac? Man, talk to me."

In a slurred voice, A.J. said, "See, my brother, I made it. How could I let you down? You're the only one who cares for me."

"Man, what are you talking about?"

"O.J., man, I blew it. I lost my good friend. He/she is gone and doesn't want to see me again."

O.J. said, "'He/she'? Man, you're tore up. What are you saying to me? Did someone die while you were in Seattle?"

"No, no, I mean he, we fell out over a business deal, ending a long-term relationship that I'll never recapture."

O.J. looked at him with a blank look on his face. "A.J., man, you're coming inside. I'm putting on some coffee; then we'll talk when you're sober." O.J. knocked on the window of the limo to get Bentley's attention. He let the glass down.

Bentley said, "Yes, Mr. O'Neil? May I help you with something?"

"Please help me get my brother inside, Bentley."

"Yes, sir. Mr. O'Neil insisted I bring him to your house."

"Not a problem, Bentley. Thank you. Please help me with him."

O.J. and Bentley held A.J. up between them as they escorted him to the basement.

"Will that be all, Mr. O'Neil?"

"Yes, Bentley, you're done for the night. Thank you. I'll see my brother home."

O.J. had to get some sense into his brother. He was worried about A.J. He hadn't seen him this drunk in years. O.J. made a pot of coffee first. Then he ran the shower. He figured if he ran some water on A.J., it would wake him; and then he'd fill him with coffee.

"OK, A.J., in the shower you go."

Still slurring, A.J. said, "Get Bentley to take me home. Nothing matters anymore."

Really angry, O.J. snapped, "Bentley is gone. I sent him home, and everything does matter. A.J. you're going to put on this bathrobe and drink this coffee. Then you're going to talk to me straight."

By 4 a.m. A. J. was full of coffee and ashamed of his actions. He wondered how much he had said to O.J. about his relationship with Dameon. He had to think quickly and cover up whatever had slipped out. O.J., sitting in the chair on the other side of the room, was waiting for A.J. to come alive. He said, "Man, you all right?"

"Yeah. I'm ashamed of myself more than anything. I apologize for coming to the house like this."

"All right, now talk to me about this friendship you lost and what got you sipping on the booze like that."

"My business associate, my close partner, we argued, and he ended our partnership."

"A.J., you never said you had a partner. I always thought you were an independent broker."

"I kept it silent because he wasn't one for the limelight. O.J., he's helped me get to where I am today. When I lost him, I lost a part of myself. We were that in tune with each other on business matters."

O.J. asked, "You said it was over business? You split up over money? A.J., you're worth millions, and from what you're telling me you're partner can't be too far behind you. So why split over money?"

A.J. couldn't tell O.J. the truth about his relationship with Dameon; that the real split was because Dameon had found a new lover in France. Dameon had wanted to meet with A.J. one last time before he committed himself to his new relationship. A.J. didn't dare tell O.J. the truth. He realized that his brother wasn't as naive as he thought, but still the time was not right. He needed to keep his life private. A.J. changed the subject. "O.J., listen, this is my problem. I'll deal with it, OK? Don't worry about me."

"I'm very worried about you. Let me talk to your business partner; reassure him that whatever differences the two of you have, you can still preserve the friendship. Let me make him realize just how good a friend you are."

"No!" A.J. said in a harsh tone. "It's my problem, and I don't care to discuss it anymore. Please, now, let's go over our plans. We don't have much time."

O.J. threw up his hands as if to say, *OK, have it your way.* "All right, A.J. I'm on your side; you gotta know that."

"I know, and thanks for taking care of me."

Westchester

9 a.m.

Ellen had overslept. She reached for the clock, saw the time and jumped out of bed. Chains couldn't hold her from picking up Dameon's luggage. What a hangover she had from the wine! She ran to the shower, rushing to make the 10 a.m. arrival time. She wanted to be at the baggage gate when the luggage came down the belt. There was no way she could make it to work today. She would call in sick; she was feeling ill. Ellen called work, and then threw on a sweatshirt and jeans. Her intention was to pick up the luggage, return home and sleep through the day so she could be fresh and alert when Dameon arrived to pick up his luggage. She thought about preparing a nice dinner and inviting him to stay. She was on a mission.

Traffic was so heavy. Ellen arrived at the airport exactly five minutes early. She parked in short-term parking and made her way to baggage claim. Dameon always flew first class, and his luggage was personalized so there was no way for her to miss it. Ellen checked the flight schedule to be sure there were no delays. The flight was on time. She was the first person at baggage claim for Flight #268. Her head was pounding from the hangover. The baggage belt began to move. She stood up close so she could grab the luggage as it came out.

Ellen waited 10 minutes before the first piece of luggage appeared, but it wasn't Dameon's. The belt turned steadily. Eventually she spotted his luggage, designer bags with his initials engraved in gold. She knew Dameon had expensive taste. Ellen removed three pieces of luggage from the belt. She couldn't believe Dameon took so much luggage for a short stay. Ellen had the valet attendant put the bags in her car. On her drive home, she kept wondering why Dameon had brought so much luggage. Ellen was curious to know what was inside. She wanted to know if she could smell Dameon's scent from the cologne he wore.

Ellen arrived home. She carried the luggage in piece by piece, and by the time she brought the last piece in, she was out of breath. She flopped down in a chair to catch her breath – meanwhile she kept looking at the luggage. A crazy thought came to her mind. What about breaking into the luggage to see what it contained? But how would she explain to Dameon about the locks being broken? She had to think quickly. Why pay money for a P.I. when she could snoop around to find things out on her own?

She looked for something to pry open the large bag. She thought she'd open the biggest one and leave the others -- this way her explanation would be justifiable. She'd tell Dameon it was damaged at the airport. Why wouldn't he believe that, the way luggage is handled? Ellen went to the kitchen to look for a screwdriver. She made her way back into the living room, and then she began to pick the lock. After two hours of picking, she finally got the lock undone.

Ellen was ashamed of what she had done, but curiosity was eating her alive. She took a deep breath before opening the bag. To her surprise, on the inside was ladies lingerie, sexier than anything she'd ever wear, perfume, wigs, dresses and makeup, all the belongings of a woman with expensive taste.

Ellen sat back down in the chair, shaking from what she had found. She wanted to know who this mystery woman was whom Dameon was keeping out of sight. Ellen thought it must be serious for him to take her on a trip using his luggage. Ellen began to cry. Tears rolled down her cheeks. First sadness then anger set in. She thought about all the long hours she had invested in trying to impress this man, and how she rushed to pick up his bags.

She felt like a big fool, a fool for love. If only he knew how she felt about him! Ellen made up her mind to take a stand. She was going to fight to unveil the truth, find out why this woman was such a well-kept secret. She looked through the bag again for more clues.

She found two pairs of size 12 women's shoes. She didn't even know women's shoes came that large. *She must be a really big woman with large feet,* Ellen thought. Why would Dameon want someone that over-sized? Dameon was 6'3" tall and very handsome. Why would he settle for that? *Maybe she's the model on the poster. She's gorgeous; maybe she just has big feet.*

Her imagination took her to places she didn't want to go, and she became very depressed. What was she to do? She couldn't tell Robin, because she'd promised her she wouldn't do anything stupid. Ellen went straight to the kitchen to pour a glass of wine. She drank and cried. Torturing her mind, she imagined Dameon in Seattle with his mystery woman. Ellen was so pissed off! *The nerve of him, calling me to pick up their luggage! I'm not one of his servants.* Ellen was furious with anger and jealousy. She drank what was left of the wine; then she lay on the sofa and cried herself to sleep.

Florida

"O.J., why are you dragging your feet? We have a plane to catch in three hours."

"I'm just feeling a little nervous about the flight, Samone. I've been up all night. I couldn't sleep."

"Ever since I told you about this trip, it's been one excuse after another. If you didn't want to go, all you had to do was say so. You've flown many times before."

"Samone, please don't start. I'm not making excuses. I'm just feeling a little sick, that's all."

Samone said sharply, "Well, take something and get over it, 'cause we are going to enjoy ourselves."

O.J. just looked at her with disgust. He was thinking about Robin arriving today, and something possibly going wrong. His mind was certainly not on Jamaica. His nerves were making him ill. Samone was making him ill. O.J. had to pull himself together. He went in the bathroom and snuck on his cell phone to call A.J.

"A.J., man, today is the day."

"Relax, bro; it's going to be fine. In a few days you'll be with Robin. Get yourself together before Samone figures out something is wrong."

"Man, I should just forget Jamaica. Tell Samone I'm leaving her. A.J., my mind won't be there."

A.J. said sarcastically, "OK, do it then. Walk out just like that. Man, keep your head cool. You're not thinking clearly. Take a deep breath. Now I want you to think about the kids. If you walk, Samone will never let you see your kids again. Man, that's no way to do it.

Go along with her plan. Pretend to have fun in Jamaica, then when you get back, your prize will be waiting for you. O.J., it will work, but you have to play your role and keep it straight with Samone."

"You're right A.J., I lost my head. Listen, I'll have my cell phone with me. Call me if anything goes wrong. Call me, please! I love this woman. Please take good care of her. Our flight leaves in two hours. Are you ready?"

"Ready as can be. Now let me get dressed so I can be on time. O.J., I got this. Don't worry. Now go so you can get back. Remember to page me with the 911 code as soon as you arrive in town, then we'll make the switch. Now go."

O.J. started to say, "But A.J.—" but he was left with a dial tone. A.J. had hung up.

A.J. took one final look at himself in the mirror. He was the spitting image of his brother. He was on his way to the airport to pick up Robin..

Westchester

Ellen lay on the couch like a corpse. She reached for the bottle of wine Dameon had given her, but there wasn't a drop left. She wanted to drown her thoughts in a bottle. She figured she'd just go to the liquor store to buy another bottle, thinking that would help her forget about Dameon. Ellen didn't realize she was developing a drinking problem. She arrived at the liquor store, rushed in to buy her bottle and headed back home. Once she entered her apartment and took another look at the luggage, she lost her cool. Ellen took the luggage and slung it across the room. She sat in the middle of the floor and poured a glass of wine. She had cared for Dameon from the day she laid eyes on him. No man had ever made her feel the way he did. Maybe no man ever would again.

Daytona Airport

A.J. stood at the arrival gate waiting for Robin to get off the plane. He took the wallet-size photo of Robin from his coat pocket to get one last peek. A.J. was very relaxed; he set his mind in focus to play his role. Robin was approaching in his direction with the biggest smile on her face.

"Hi, baby!" A.J./O.J. said, reaching out to hug Robin. "How was the flight?"

Robin said, "Hi, sweetheart. I made it! I'm here! The flight was good."

A.J./O.J. said, "Stand back and let me take a good look at you. Honey, you look good enough to drive a crazy man wild. Let me kiss you."

Robin, still smiling from ear to ear, said, "O.J., you're looking good yourself. I can't help but notice something is different, though. Maybe it's been so long since we've seen each other. No kissing just yet. Remember, I'm here to help you. I don't want to get your heart rate going too fast."

A.J./O.J. said, "Robin, I know it's been too long. I'm wearing the patches now, but in a few days I'll make all this up to you. Let me at least hold your hand. What harm can that do?"

Robin said, "OK, Mr. O'Neil, just hand holding. How have you been?"

A.J./O.J. said, "Missing you more than you know. I'm fine now. Listen, are you hungry?"

"I could eat a bite."

"Good, I've got a day planned for us. We'll bring the luggage to our hotel, get something to eat, and then I'll show you off around town."

Robin laughed. "Show me off, huh?"

"Yes, show you off. You're the most beautiful woman in Florida, and I want the men to stare at my woman. Take a look, 'cause she's all mine."

A.J. and Robin picked up her luggage and headed for the hotel. He couldn't believe how gorgeous Robin was in person. The picture he had didn't do her justice. He played his role very well; she had bought it, and she couldn't tell the difference. A.J. was ready to show her some of his charm. Not only was Robin very attractive, but she smelled fantastic. He could see what his brother saw in her. A.J. sensed she had a warm personality and was very affectionate.

They held hands on the drive to the hotel. A.J. had flowers delivered to the room in an assortment of colors and styles to welcome Robin. He had selected a beach-front resort. He wanted to leave a lasting impression with Robin and wanted to make O.J. shine. A.J. had a line of women's summer wear delivered to the room, waiting for Robin. His connections with Dameon, the world-famous designer, allowed him to have access to the latest women's clothing, free of charge. He wanted O.J. to be impressed with what he'd done when he returned from Jamaica.

A.J. had a full day scheduled -- lunch overlooking the ocean, a full day at the spa, then a lovely evening dancing. He had even arranged a boat tour of the Florida shore for the next day.

These were some of his personal preferences being displayed. A.J. had money, and he believed in the finer things in life. Entertaining was his specialty, and cost was never an issue. He tried to keep it simple so as not to make Robin think he had used all of O.J's life savings. She'd wonder how a man of O.J.'s stature could afford such luxuries. A.J. was ready to answer any questions she had. All he wanted to do was to show her a memorable time. They arrived at the beach house.

Robin said, "O.J., this is lovely and right on the beach."

A.J./O.J. said, "I'm glad you like it. You take the key and go inside while I get our bags."

Robin opened the door to a room full of beautiful floral arrangements. She'd never seen so many flowers at once except in a garden. She stood there for a second in disbelief. A.J. entered with the bags, and Robin ran to embrace him with a huge hug.

"O.J., honey, thank you. They're beautiful. How thoughtful of you." She began to cry, tears rolling down her cheeks.

"Robin, did I do something wrong? Why are you crying?"

Robin wiped her tears. "No, honey, it's just that no one has ever welcomed me in this manner. Never have I had so many flowers at one time."

Robin walked toward A.J. and gave him a kiss. A.J., not resisting the moment, for a second forgot why he was there. The kiss was so touching he couldn't help but respond. A.J. pulled himself away from Robin very quickly.

"Honey, remember the testing. I can't get too excited, but I must say that kiss was well worth the flowers and more."

"O.J., I'm sorry. I forgot for a moment about the testing. All the flowers excited me."

"Baby, I understand. Why don't you freshen up, and then we'll get a bite to eat and do a little sightseeing?"

"That sounds good. I'm going to change into something cooler."

"Speaking of cooler, sweetheart, in the closet you'll find a few summer outfits I've selected for you. I'd like to see you in them while you're here."

"O.J., you didn't! All this must have cost you a fortune." Robin gave him another hug.

"All right, baby, enough of that." He put her hands down to her side. "You deserve all of it and more. Now, you freshen up while I go gas up the car."

"O.J., you're the best! I love you."

A.J. just looked at her. He had a hard time dealing with those words.

A.J./O.J. said, "The feeling is mutual. Now freshen up; I'll be back in a few."

A.J. went to the car, which had a full tank of gas. He realized that his plan would be harder than he imagined. Robin was very affectionate and sexy on top of it; how was he going to keep his emotions intact? A.J. was attracted to her. He had a problem. He had two days and nights to be with Robin. A.J. had never allowed any woman other than his sister Diane to affect him emotionally. He wouldn't allow any woman so close. A.J. sat in the car to collect his thoughts. He remembered the words he had said to his brother O.J. in a moment of weakness. Master of the Game…in other words, mind control over matter. A.J. had to keep his mind focused on his purpose of playing the role of his brother. A.J. started the car and took a drive around the block. He gave Robin enough time to freshen up, and himself enough time to get his head straight.

Jamaica

"O.J. isn't it beautiful? Aren't you glad we came? Jamaica is a lovely honeymoon spot."

"Yes, Samone, just happy to be here."

"Do you ever think about marriage, O.J.?"

"Marriage, Samone? Where is that coming from?"

"Well, O.J., maybe it's the atmosphere. We have been together long enough to finalize it. Make it right before God. Surprise the kids."

"Samone, this is supposed to be a vacation. We didn't come all the way to Jamaica to be married."

"You're right, O.J. If you put it that way, I can make wedding plans when we get back home. A nice intimate wedding with both families."

"Samone, don't go putting words into my mouth. I said nothing about a wedding, be it here in Jamaica or back home. Let me be the one to ask you. Don't back me into a corner. Where in the world is all this coming from, and why now?"

"O.J., we've spent all these years together. You gave me an engagement ring years ago, and it stopped there. I think we both need to think about our future."

"Samone, I can't deal with this right now. I'm going for a walk."

"Fine, O.J., but when will you deal with it? I got us the honeymoon suite; why not deal with it now?" As he walked away, Samone was screaming at the top of her lungs.

O.J. walked out on her, slamming the door behind him. He was furious. The last thing he wanted to hear from Samone was talk of marriage. O.J's mind was in Florida, wondering how things were going with Robin and A.J. This Jamaica thing was turning into a nightmare.

Westchester

Dameon looked at his limo driver. "Raymond, would you phone Ms. Ellen? I need to go by her place to retrieve my luggage."

"Yes, Mr. Davenport."

Ellen picked up the phone. "Hello?"

Raymond said, "Phone call from Mr. Davenport, ma'am; please hold."

Dameon said, "Hi, Ellen, I just arrived at the airport, and I'm en route to your house. Is this a good time for you?"

"Dameon, I'm afraid not. May I please bring the luggage to you later this evening? I'm a bit under the weather, and I need to shower, dress, and bring myself to life."

"Ellen, I'm sorry to hear you're not feeling well. Is there anything I can get for you? Your voice sounds terribly weak. Don't worry about delivering the bags this evening. I'll have Raymond pick them up tomorrow."

"That will be fine, Dameon. I'm just not feeling up to company. Please don't take it personally."

"Ellen, are you sure I can't do anything? Are you going to be all right alone?"

"I'm fine, Dameon!" Ellen said very curtly.

"Thank you for picking up the luggage, Ellen. If you need anything, anything at all, please don't hesitate to call, and that's an order. I'll let you go. I'll call you later."

"Good bye, Dameon."

Ellen was hung-over and angry with Dameon. His voice didn't excite her. She had to come up with an explanation for the broken luggage. She wasn't ready to face him. Ellen dragged herself to the bathroom to turn on the shower. She walked past the door-length mirror; the way she looked frightened her. Her makeup was smeared from falling asleep on the sofa, and her hair was a mess. She needed a complete body makeover. Then there was the super-size headache she had from the wine.

She took a good look in the mirror, talking to herself "I am not going to let Dameon emotionally badger my mind. He's got to know how I feel about him after I explain the broken luggage. He's just so cute, and he should be mine, not belong to some big-foot Amazon freak. I'm going to fight for my man!"

Somehow Ellen knew she had to muster up the strength to fight this mystery woman. "May the best woman win!" she said. Then into the shower she went.

Florida

A.J./O.J. arrived back at the beach house. Robin had ordered a bottle of champagne from the front desk.

"O.J., honey, I felt a toast was in order in honor of our finally being together. I'll drink for both of us. It's not a good idea for you to drink until your tests are complete."

A.J./O.J. said, "Robin, honey, I'm sure a little won't hurt."

Robin poured a small glass for him. "O.J., thank you so much for the beautiful clothes. They're lovely, and I know they're very expensive. Everything fits perfectly. Let me model for you. You sit and relax and let me do my thing."

A.J. sat comfortably in a lounge chair. Robin turned on the radio to smooth jazz. A.J was wondering how O.J. was doing in Jamaica. He wanted O.J. to know he had everything under control so that he could relax and not show Samone how tense he was.

Robin came out of the bathroom in a canary red two-piece swimsuit which showed off every inch of her well-proportioned body. A.J. couldn't help but stare at her. It was almost as if she were tempting his sexuality. A.J. got to his feet.

A.J./O.J. said, "Baby, you're wearing that. It looks really nice on you. The color becomes you."

Robin began turning around in circles. "Honey, for your eyes only. Thank you. I love it."

A.J./O.J said, "Good. Now get dressed so I can feed you. This is too tempting for me, Robin."

"O.J., I'm so sorry. I didn't mean it in that way. I just wanted you to see how well everything fits. Let me put something else on. I'm so sorry."

A.J./O.J. said, "I'm going to wait out by the water and get a bit of fresh air."

"OK O.J. I'll be right out."

A.J. needed to slip away out of Robin's sight for a second. He wanted to leave a message on O.J's phone to assure him everything was going well. He walked away from the beach house along the shore.

O.J.'s voice mail answered. "Hi, I can't take your call; please leave a message."

"O.J., man, this is A.J. I got to make this quick. Everything is fine. She doesn't suspect a thing. She's very happy, and pretty, too.

Man, I got everything under control. So relax and try to enjoy Jamaica. Later."

A.J. worried about his brother's happiness; he wanted O.J. to rest his mind.

When he came back to the beach house, Robin asked, "Is this more like it?" She was dressed in a sheer two-piece skirt set.

"Robin, you look lovely, and you smell so good. I've picked a great place for us to dine. Hope you're hungry."

"Starving is more like it!" She took his arm and they walked to the car.

A.J. had taken a serious liking to Robin. She was warm, and her smile did something to him. It reminded him of his mother.

Jamaica

O.J. checked his phone messages. He listened to the message his brother had left and was relieved everything was going smoothly. He headed back to the hotel to deal with Samone.

"Samone, look," he said. "I'm sorry I stormed out on you. It's just that all this is happening so fast."

"All of what, O.J.?"

"First the trip, and now this talk of marriage."

"O.J., we've been together all these years. Don't you think it's time to legalize our living arrangements? God forbid something happens to you. What would become of me and the kids?"

"Samone, if that's what you're worried about, you need not be. I've made provisions if something should happen. You all will be well taken care of."

"Do you love me, O.J.?"

O.J. looked away for a second. "Yes, Samone. How could I not feel something for you? You're the mother of my children."

"O.J., I realize we haven't been as close as a couple should be over the years. When you were away, it made me realize just how much you really mean to me. I missed you so." She walked closer to O.J.

"I missed you and the kids, too."

"So let's try to mend what was lost. That's why I planned this trip for us, O.J. Can we both work together on this?"

"Samone, I'll try, but don't back me into a corner. Marriage is so final, and I'm not ready to discuss that now."

"Final? What do you mean by that, O.J.? You've spent half your life with me. Are you having second thoughts about the rest?"

"Samone, let's not argue. Let's try to work together, not against each other. How about a swim in the pool?" he suggested, changing the subject.

Westchester

Ellen took one last look at herself in the full-length mirror. She was gorgeous. She was ready to pay Dameon a surprise visit. She'd spent half the afternoon at the beauty salon getting a full makeover. The dress she chose was so tight it showed every curve. She wanted Dameon to see what he was missing. For her finishing touch, she sprayed her favorite perfume. Ellen thought she'd take an aggressive approach; boldness was her friend. She strode out the door, ready to catch her man.

On the drive to Dameon's, she took a few sips of wine. With the top down on her convertible, Will Downey playing on the CD player, she was a woman on the move and with a mission. Ellen was turning the heads of men passing her on the expressway. She looked straight ahead with one thing in mind, getting to Dameon.

Ellen arrived at Dameon's house. She boldly walked to the door and rang the bell.

Dameon opened it himself. "Why, Ellen, what a surprise! Please come in."

"Hello, Dameon. I was in the neighborhood, and I wanted to explain something to you about the luggage."

She took one look at Dameon dressed in his silk robe, and all of her boldness went out the window. This man mesmerized her with his penetrating eyes.

"Ellen, you look stunning for someone who was ill. Do you have a date?"

"As a matter of fact, I do, Dameon. We're meeting for cocktails."

"Lucky fella. You're a sight for sore eyes, and I like that perfume. What's the name of it?"

"It's Chameleon, by Dave Pier."

"Smells great, Ellen. Now about the luggage --?"

"I forgot to make mention to you that one of the locks had been damaged. Apparently it was damaged en route. I filed a claim with the airport. It slipped my mind, and I forgot to tell you earlier when you called."

"It's no big concern, as long as there isn't anything missing. I've got plenty of luggage. But I appreciate your taking care of the problem. In fact, did you happen to bring the luggage with you?"

Ellen said, "No, I was just passing through the neighborhood on my way to meet my friend, and I wanted to tell you about the accident. I apologize for dropping in."

"That was very thoughtful of you, Ellen. I'll send Raymond to fetch my bags tomorrow, if that's not a problem. No apology needed; you're always welcome."

"That will be fine, Dameon." She was staring at his masculine body.

"Ellen, may I offer you a drink before you meet your date?"

"Yes, I'd like that, Dameon."

Dameon brought Ellen into the den. Ellen wanted so desperately to kiss him. Dameon turned his back to prepare the drinks. Ellen studied him from behind, her imagination getting the best of her.

"Ellen, might I make a suggestion without your being offended?"

"Why sure, Dameon."

"That is a lovely after-five dress, but it would look more elegant if you wore your hair up."

Ellen couldn't believe he took that much of an interest in her. "May I use a mirror to put it up?" she asked.

"We can do better than that. Bring your drink, follow me to the dressing room, and I'll do that for you. I don't want you to unravel yourself. You're way too pretty for that tonight."

Dameon took Ellen by the hand and escorted her to the dressing room. He put a smock over her dress, and he went to work. Ellen was like butter in her chair. Dameon ran his long fingers through her hair. Ellen put her head back, closed her eyes and imagined him caressing the rest of her body. She was completely relaxed. Dameon pinned her hair in a French twist with dainty curls hanging on the side. She was breathtaking by the time he finished. Little did he know it was all for him. There was no date.

"Ellen, open your eyes; look in the mirror."

"It's gorgeous, Dameon. Where did you learn to do hair?"

"I have my secrets, and you have yours. I'll never tell. Your date will be impressed."

Ellen turned to Dameon and, looking him straight in the eye, boldly kissed him on the cheek. "Thank you so much, Dameon."

"You're so welcome. Now you'd better get going. No man likes to be kept waiting too long."

"Yeah, you're right," she said with hesitation in her voice. She wasn't ready to leave him. She headed for the door, only to turn around as if she'd forgotten something.

"Dameon, I wanted to tell you something else before I leave."

"Yes, Ellen, what is it?" He asked, his dark eyes gazing at her.

She looked into his dark penetrating eyes and froze. Boldness had died. She said, "Don't forget we have a 7 a.m. meeting in the morning."

Dameon smiled. "Don't you forget. You're the one with the date. Now go knock him dead. Have a lovely evening, Ellen."

"Thanks, Dameon. I plan on it, and thanks for the hairdo. Good night."

Dameon said, "Good night. Be safe."

Ellen got into her car and drove a few blocks, but was forced to pull over because her tears and sobbing were uncontrollable.

Florida

"O.J., Florida is beautiful. I could get used to this weather. I'm so glad I came."

A.J./O.J. said, "I'm glad you came, too. We're having dinner at the oceanfront grill."

"Do you recall the first time we met, how we danced? I feel like dancing tonight O.J."

"Oh yes, I sure do remember our first dance. How we held each other close. We'll go dancing after dinner." A.J. was glad he remembered everything O.J. had shared with him.

"I love you, O.J."

"Me, too. I feel the same."

Robin looked at him funny. That was the first time he hadn't said he loved her in return. It made her feel a little awkward.

"Are you all right?"

"I'm fine, Robin. Is there something wrong?"

"It's OK. It's just probably me. Let's go inside to order dinner."

They went inside the restaurant. This was one of A.J's regular hangouts, and he was well known at this restaurant. He had a table reserved especially for him overlooking the ocean.

The hostess said, "Good evening, Mr. O'Neil. Would you like your usual table?"

"Yes, thank you." He and Robin sat at the table.

"Do you come here quite often?"

"On occasion, with my brother, the other O'Neil."

Robin looked surprised. "You never mentioned you had a brother."

"We're not that close."

"He wouldn't happen to be that rich tycoon real estate broker, would he?" Robin asked.

"The one and only. How would you know of him, Robin?"

"I don't. But one of my girlfriends was inquiring about him when she found out I was seeing you. She put the two last names together, associating you both with Florida. She said she met your brother at a social function."

A.J./O.J. said, "That would be my brother. Always in the spotlight, a regular social butterfly."

Robin asked, "What happened to your relationship? You said you weren't close."

"Robin, honey, please, I really don't care to talk about it."

"I understand."

"How's your son and your girlfriend Ellen?"

"Oh my, I forgot to call Ellen. Honey, remind me to call her tonight. They can't wait to meet you. In fact, I was thinking of giving a party in the next few months, and you'll be my guest of honor. I want to show you off."

A.J./O.J. said, "I wouldn't miss it for the world."

Robin reached for O.J.'s hand. "That's what I love about you most; you want to see me happy."

A.J. looked deep into Robin's eyes. He saw in her something he hadn't seen in years. A woman truly loving her man. He realized why O.J. was in a dilemma. He had spent all of those years with Samone and the kids, and now there was this beautiful, warm intelligent woman who loved the hell out of him. O.J. had a mess on his hands. A.J. just stared at Robin.

"Honey, are you feeling OK? You're looking at me so strange."

A.J./O.J. said, "I'm just so glad you're here. I just can't believe it."

"O.J., I want so badly for you to kiss me, to make love to me. This is harder than I thought. I know it's not easy for you, either."

"I'm trying not to think about it. Why don't we order our food?" he suggested, quickly changing the subject.

"Where are your kids?"

"They're spending the weekend with their mom."

"I hope someday I'll get to meet them."

"Sure, honey that will all come with time."

"I know, O.J. You do love me, don't you?"

"Why of course I do, Robin, without a doubt."

"It's just that you haven't said it once since I've been here."

"Haven't I?"

"No, you haven't. I first noticed when I said it to you. Has anything changed?" Robin asked innocently.

251

"Of course not!" He reached for her hand. "I love you! I love you! I love you, Robin. See, I can't stop repeating it!"

A.J. couldn't believe those words had rolled so easily off his lips. He had vowed never to say those three words again after losing his mother. Robin was the only person who was able to bring it out of him. He had a different look in his eye towards her. Suddenly she meant more to him than someone he could play games with. A.J. began to feel ashamed of himself. Now he realized what his brother meant by "She's not just anyone." In a matter of hours of being with this woman, he had opened up his heart to feelings. A.J. got up from the table and excused himself.

"Robin, please excuse me while I go to the men's room. I'm feeling ill all of a sudden. Just give me a minute. I'm sorry."

Robin sat at the table puzzled by O.J.'s sudden illness and wondering if he'd been ill all along, and he'd just been putting on a good show for her. She felt something wasn't right. She sat alone for 20 minutes.

Meanwhile A.J. was in the lounge drinking a shot of cognac. He couldn't believe after all these years the last woman he'd said those words to was his mom. A.J. was puzzled, wondering what made Robin so different. He felt it was something about her smile. A.J. for the first time in a long time lost control of his emotions. He downed another shot and then went back to the table.

Robin wasn't there. He assumed she was in the ladies room. He asked the hostess if she'd seen the woman he was with. The hostess told him she had left in a cab.

A.J. panicked. Twice in one night, within minutes, his emotions had been torn down by this woman. He paid for the meal and ran to the car. He assumed Robin was headed back to the beach house. *Where else could she have gone?* He wondered, *She knows nothing about Florida.* Worried that something might happen to her, A.J. raced for time, running red lights. How could he explain to O.J., after he had left Robin in his care, if something happened to her? *Why did I leave her?* He asked himself.

Robin didn't know the city, but she remembered the name of the beachfront hotel and told the cab driver to take her there. She was upset with O.J. Their communication was apparently stronger at a distance. If he wasn't feeling well, why would he have hidden it from her? She needed to be alone, to think about what to do. She thought she'd check into a different hotel and leave O.J. a note. Maybe she was over-reacting. Just as the cab driver pulled up to the door of the beach house, A.J.'s car pulled up behind them. Honking his horn, he jumped out of the car, grabbed Robin and hugged her tight.

"Robin, are you all right? Why did you leave like that? You scared me. My heart can't take this."

"O.J., I'm sorry. I forgot about the testing. I was upset. I thought you were making a mockery of your love for me, the way you repeatedly said it. I thought you were making fun of it, taking it lightly." Tears ran down her face.

"No, no! I didn't mean it that way at all." Hands trembling, he reached for his handkerchief to wipe her face. "Robin, I am so sorry. I love you. Please know that, please forgive me. I never meant to make you cry." A.J., not pretending at this point, meant every word he said to her.

Robin said, "Let me pay the cab driver and send him on his way. We'll go inside and talk this out."

A.J. forgot about his role-playing, forgot about O.J. and let his guard down. He was getting attached to her.

Jamaica

"That was a good swim. Would you like to have dinner out or would you like for me to call room service O.J.?"

"Whatever you want to do is fine with me." He was preoccupied with thoughts of Robin and not paying attention to what Samone was talking about.

Samone ordered dinner in. She figured they'd have a romantic dinner on the terrace of their room; she had a lovely evening planned for the two of them. Why not enjoy the honeymoon suite? Noticing O.J. was quiet, she asked, "A penny for your thoughts."

"Did you just say something, Samone?"

"Yeah, I did. Where are you, O.J.? You're certainly not here with me. I've ordered dinner, and we'll be eating on the terrace."

"Anything you want, Samone." He was looking off into the distance from the terrace.

"Yes – there is something I want, O.J. I want for you to act more enthused about being here. Kiss me."

"Samone, I should call home and have A.J. check in on the kids," he said, still avoiding her.

"O.J., the kids are fine. Kiss me."

O.J. heard her the first time. He didn't feel romantic.

"Samone, listen, can we think about the romance later, like after dinner? We just got here. Give me time to adjust to Jamaica."

"O.J., I didn't bring you here to stare out into the sunset or stay locked up in the room. What seems to be the problem? Is this about us or is it someone else?"

O.J. looked guilty. "Samone, there's no problem. We have no problems, and there's no one else. Why would you ever think such a thing?"

"It's your actions, O.J. You seem so distant."

O J. had made up his mind. He'd better do whatever Samone wanted him to do; she was starting to suspect something.

"Samone," he suggested, "why don't you change into something sexy? You want me to be romantic, then help me out."

Samone went into the bathroom to freshen up. O.J. snuck out his cell phone while she was in the shower. He called A.J. and left a message on his voice mail.

"A.J., I received your message. Man, I'm so restless. I can't get into this. Samone is getting on my nerves. She's starting to suspect something. She asked if there was someone else. I have to get the situation here under control. I'm relieved to know you've got it all handled there. Isn't Robin a sight for sore eyes? Be good man. I'll see you soon. Thanks. Later."

Samone came out of the bathroom wearing a bright orange thong and matching bra. O.J. had his back turned, standing on the terrace.

"O.J., come here, baby."

O.J. turned to face her. He couldn't believe his eyes. Samone had never been so provocative in all their years together. She would always wear his shirts to bed, nothing so revealing. O.J. couldn't believe what he was seeing. Two kids and 20 plus years later, she still had a shape out of this world. She had just kept it hidden from him until recently.

O.J. said, "Wow, Samone! You look –"

Samone covered his mouth with her hand. "Don't say it, O.J. Just show me."

Westchester

Ellen sat in her car, head on the steering wheel, makeup running down her cheeks from her tears. She had lost all track of time. Suddenly there was a knock on the car window; it was Dameon.

"Ellen, are you all right? I noticed your car parked on the side of the rode as I was driving by."

Ellen's heart was pounding. Caught off guard, she began to wipe the tears away so Dameon couldn't see them "Oh, Dameon, I'm fine. I was just reaching for my cell phone. My date had an emergency, so we'll have to take a rain-check."

"Thank God! You scared the heck out of me. I spotted your car so I backed up. I wanted to make sure you were all right. Sorry about your date. You look so lovely; it's his loss," Dameon consoled her.

"I'm OK. Thanks, Dameon."

"No, you're not. You're too pretty to let this evening go to waste. I was on my way to Lamarage for dinner. Would you care to join me? I'd love to have a beautiful woman like you with me."

Ellen looked up at Dameon; her eyes lit up.

"Yes, I'd like that, Dameon, very much."

"Ellen, your makeup is smeared. Have you been crying, dear?"

Ellen, put on the spot, couldn't tell Dameon she was crying over him. "Oh, no, it's my allergies, driving with my convertible top down and all the pollen in the air. You know how allergies can be."

Dameon played it off. He knew she had been crying. He knew how matters of the heart and broken dates can make a girl teary-eyed. He'd had plenty of disappointments in his day, most of them from Aaron O'Neil. For a moment he reflected back to all the broken dates with A.J., and he knew exactly how Ellen felt.

"Yeah, Ellen, I know. Allergies can mess a girl up. Let's take your car back to the house, get your makeup freshened up, and then we can be on our way."

Ellen was on cloud nine. A real date with Dameon, without work. She was sure glad she had stopped on the side of the road. Dameon followed her back to his house. Like a gentleman, he got out of his car, opened her door, took her hand and escorted her into the house. She couldn't help noticing what a sharp dresser Dameon was with his Stacy Adams shoes on. He took Ellen to the dressing room to fix her make-up, and he re-did her hair.

Dameon said, "Ellen, now you look like new money. Shall we?" he asked, holding his arm out for hers.

Ellen thought she'd died and gone to heaven. The man she adored was on her arm. She was all smiles. She wondered where his mystery woman was tonight. She certainly wasn't on his arm. Off they went in his Bentley to Lamarage.

Florida

"Robin, I'm so sorry I left you like that. Please forgive me."

"Is everything all right with us, O.J.? Are you feeling all right?"

"Honey, I'm fine, really. Everything is fine. Look, you've had a long day, and I know you're hungry. Let me make this up to you, please. I'll order delivery service from the best restaurant I know. You just lie down and relax."

"I'm OK with that, but are you sure we're all right?"

A.J./O.J. looked her in the eye. "Yes, Robin. I love you. If it means anything, I wasn't making a mockery of our love."

Robin walked toward A.J., put her arms around him and romantically kissed him. They both got caught up in the kiss. A.J., not letting go of her, lost himself in Robin's arms. Her kiss was so sexual, warm, and heartfelt, he forgot his role playing. Quickly he jumped back.

"Robin, forgive me. I lost myself for a minute," A.J. said, literally meaning every word.

"O.J., you kissed me as if it was our first kiss. Are you sure everything is OK?"

"Yes, Robin, everything is fine. Now let me get some food in you. I'm going to order the biggest lobster dinner you've ever had. Why don't you get comfortable while I go to the front desk to get the number to call? I'll be back in a few."

"OK, but please don't be long."

"I promise I'll be right back."

He got beyond their room door and leaned his head against it. He couldn't believe how caught up in that kiss he had gotten. He was feeling sexually attracted to Robin, and it frightened him. He was feeling something for his brother's woman. A.J. wanted Robin sexually. The game had turned out to be a trick on him. He never thought his feelings would be drawn to Robin. A.J. was no longer role-playing; he was falling in love with Robin, and he didn't know what to do about it.

He walked to the front office to clear his head. He knew the restaurant number by heart, but he needed time away from Robin to resist the temptation. He wanted her just as much as his brother did, and there was nothing he could do but play his role.

Jamaica

O.J. and Samone lay in bed after making love.

"O.J., you are awesome -- that was great. Hey, by the way, there's something I've been meaning to tell you."

"Yes, Samone, what might that be?"

"I stopped taking the pill. I figure a baby would be good for us. Then we could be married before the baby is born," Samone said innocently.

O.J. jumped out of bed. "Samone, we don't need any more children. How dare you stop taking the pill without discussing it with me! I don't want any more kids. I don't want to get married! I didn't want this trip!"

O.J. blew up. He'd had enough of Samone and her wild plans.

"I'm afraid it's no longer what you want, O.J. If you don't decide to make a legal woman out of me, you can forget about me and the kids. If I get pregnant, we'll just be starting over."

"Samone, what's gotten into you? You can't force me, nor will I let you use the kids against me. Why are you doing this?"

"I've been with you all these years, O.J., and I know you better than you know yourself. Ever since you've come back from Westchester, you've been acting differently. I don't know what happened there, but I do know one thing: we are going to be married or I'm out, me and the kids, for good."

O.J. didn't argue with her; instead he got up and left the room. He was furious. He knew Samone suspected something. He had just blown it big time. What if she is pregnant? He felt as though his life was out of control. Trying to smooth things over to get back in Samone's good graces, he went to the front desk of the hotel to order flowers and champagne to be sent to their room. He needed that one night with Robin once he returned to figure everything out.

O.J. was angry, but he had to role-play just like his brother. He figured if he gave Samone a romantic evening, she'd forget all the things he had said to her. He thought about what his brother had said to him about being master of the game.

Westchester

"Ellen, it's too bad your date cancelled out. You look absolutely stunning tonight."

"Thank you, Dameon. Lamarage is so cozy. Do you often dine here?"

"Yes, as a matter of fact, I do. You know, Ellen, I just realized we've always talked business. I can't say that I know anything on a personal level about you. Tell me, have you lived in Westchester all your life?"

Ellen, her hands sweating, thought Dameon was taking a serious interest in her. "Yes, Dameon, I was born and raised right here in Westchester."

"And the young man you were meeting for cocktails, is he your man?"

"Oh no, by no means, Dameon. He is just a friend."

"I ask because everyone desires to have that special someone in their lives." He was gazing at her with his deep black eyes.

"Yes, you're right. What about you? Is there a special someone in your life?"

"There was, but we've decided to keep it on a friendship level. My schedule demands so much of my time. There's really no one, nor a solid relationship."

"Dameon, could it be you haven't found that special someone yet? Sometimes things can be right at our feet and we miss them." She was trying to tell Dameon how she felt.

"You're absolutely right, Ellen. I believe in exploring my options. For now I feel I'm where I should be in my life. I have a successful business, health, money in the bank. What more can a person ask for?"

"Do you ever get lonely, Dameon?"

"Why, certainly not. I have enough on my plate to keep me occupied."

"How was Seattle? Did you travel alone or did you meet with friends?" Ellen inquired.

"Seattle was lovely, and of course I have plenty of friends there. The flight was long, but the stay was well worth it. I purchased some property while I was there. A good friend is into real estate and talked me into buying a house there."

"Oh, a good friend? So I imagine you'll be spending a lot of time in Seattle." She was thinking that the mystery woman lived in Seattle.

"It's a possibility. Ellen, I can't help but notice that the two gentlemen at the table across from us keep looking over at us. Would you care to send them a drink over? You may get lucky and meet that someone special."

"Dameon, I'd rather not leave the door open. I'm sort of feeling my way out on someone I admire."

Dameon said, "Is that a fact? Do tell; who's the lucky guy?"

Ellen eyes were as big as tea cups from being put on the spot. She couldn't tell him. She was speechless.

"Dameon, I have my secrets, and you have yours," she said finally. They both laughed.

Florida

"Robin, dinner will be delivered within the hour. How about a game of chess?"

"I'd like that. O.J., that handkerchief you gave me outside had 'Dameon' written on it. Is that a new brand name?"

A.J. looked nervous; he'd forgotten where he'd gotten the hanky. Dameon must have slipped it in his jacket pocket for a keepsake, as a remembrance of him and Seattle.

"No, it's not a name brand. Dameon is a good friend. I borrowed the hanky from him. In fact, he's the designer I purchased your summer wear from. He's a very dear friend. Robin, have you ever met someone for the first time in your life and felt as if you've known that person forever?"

"Yes, O.J. That's exactly how I felt when we met."

"Well, that's how it was when I met Dameon."

Robin said, "Some people have that effect on you. How about that game of chess?"

Jamaica

"The flowers are so pretty. Thank you, O.J." Samone seemed to be softening.

"Samone, listen, I apologize for the things I said to you. Let's just try to have a good time while we're here."

"O.J., were you really serious about not wanting any more kids? What if I get pregnant?"

O.J. kept his voice even, trying not to display his anger. "Samone, we'll deal with it if it happens. I just want to enjoy our time together without stressing over things that have yet to occur."

"You're right, O.J." She walked towards him to kiss him.

The two days in Jamaica flew by. Samone was very happy. O.J. tried to make it a memorable trip for her, although his mind was in Florida. Finally it was time to go home -- O.J. couldn't wait to see Robin. He gently reminded Samone of the trip he was to take with A.J. to Atlanta.

"Samone, honey, let's pick up the kids on our way home. But remember, I've gotta leave with A.J. this afternoon to bring the cars to the auction."

"We just got back in town. What's the hurry? Don't you at least want to spend time with the kids O.J.?"

"You knew about this trip with A.J. Please let's not argue over it. Didn't you enjoy yourself in Jamaica?"

"Yes, I did. Very much."

"So what's the problem now? A.J. and I are only going to be gone overnight. He already booked an afternoon flight, and I'll be back before you realize I'm gone."

O.J. was rushing to get to Robin. He took Samone and the kids home and headed straight to A.J's place to await the switch.

Beach House

"Robin, these past two days with you have been heaven," A.J./O.J. said, expressing his true feelings towards her.

"O.J., kiss me just once. It's so hard to hold back," Robin pleaded.

A.J. took her in his arms and held her as close as he could. He kissed her with passion. His last few minutes with Robin were soon to end once he received the page from O.J. A.J. looked deeply into her eyes.

"Robin, I'm in love with you. I love you." From the depth of his soul, he was able to tell Robin he loved her, because it was true. He really had fallen in love with her.

"O.J., now I know you do. I feel your love. I love you, too."

"Just let me hold you close in my arms. I want to savor this moment and keep it fresh in my heart forever, Robin." He held onto her as if he would never see her again. And then his pager went off with the 911 code.

Westchester

"Ellen, would you care to dance?"

Ellen was getting nervous. She was finally getting a chance to be close to him. "Yes, I'd like that, Dameon."

As they walked towards the dance floor, the two men who had been sitting across the room were staring at Dameon. One gentleman came up behind Dameon and introduced himself.

"Please excuse me. I don't mean to interrupt you all, but haven't we met?" he asked Dameon.

Dameon said, "It's a possibility. I remember faces but lose track of names."

"My name is Mark," the stranger said. "We met at a club in Seattle. Do you remember?"

Dameon tried to brush him off so Ellen wouldn't pick up on the conversation. He had met Mark in a gay bar in Seattle.

Dameon said, "I'm sorry, I'm afraid you have me mixed up with someone else. But please, let me give you my business card if you're ever in the need of designer clothing." Dameon handed Mark the card with his private phone numbers on it. On the back of the card it read: "Call me later; we'll get together."

Mark read the card and played it off. "I'm terribly sorry, sir. Thank you for your card."

Dameon said, "My pleasure."

"Dameon, you are so popular. Are you frequently mistaken for someone else?"

He smiled. "People always seem to come up to me for some reason. They use that same old tired line. 'Haven't we met before?' Knowing they never knew me. That's one of the oldest lines in the book."

Out on the dance floor a slow melody was playing, and Dameon pulled Ellen close to him. She laid her head on his broad chest, closed her eyes and got a good sniff of his expensive cologne. She thought she'd died and came back to life. She was in Dameon's arms at last.

Dameon was thinking about A.J. This very song was their theme song. Oh how he longed to hear A.J.'s voice. Dameon realized the break-up was causing him a lot of stress. Maybe he had done the wrong thing – breaking it off with A.J. in the hopes of forcing his hand into committing to him.

A.J. had a variety of people he saw on the regular, and Dameon had wanted him all to himself. To get even, Dameon led A.J. to believe he had gotten involved with someone in France. Dameon was playing hard to get, but hurting himself in the process. The longer the song played, the more he needed to hear A.J.'s voice.

"Please let's stop, Ellen. I have to make an important phone call."

Back at the table, Ellen was looking sad, wondering why he stopped in the middle of the song. Her imagination was getting the best of her. Maybe he had to call his mystery woman.

Florida Beach House

"Robin, honey, my pager just went off. Remember I told you I was on call for work? Well, I just received a page. I have to report in and make sure everything is running smoothly, and then I'll be right back. Trust me -- I don't want to leave you. Just let me hold you close before I go."

"O.J., what's wrong? You're holding me as if you're not coming back. I understand duty calls, but I'll be here when you return."

"I know, Robin. I've got to get going. How about one more kiss for the road?" A.J. liked the way she kissed him and the warm feeling it gave him.

Robin laughed. "OK, honey, now get going before you lose your job. I promise you I'll be here when you return."

A.J. didn't want to leave her. He was in love with her, but he knew he had to get to O.J.

"All right, Robin, I'm out of here. Give me that smile before I go."

Robin looked at him strangely with a smirk on her face, as if to say, 'What is going on?'

"Robin, I love you. Hold onto that until I come back."

"I will."

A.J. walked out, closing the door behind him. He drove around the corner and parked. He had to get his composure together before he met with O.J. He had to deal with his feelings. He wiped the lipstick off his lips and then phoned his house where he knew O.J. would be waiting.

"O.J., man, it's me. Pick up the phone."

There was excitement in O.J.'s voice "What's wrong A.J.?"

"Everything is fine. I'm on my way. I told Robin work was paging me."

"A.J., man, thank you -- I owe you so much."

"I'll be there soon," A.J. assured him.

He was torn between his love for O.J. and his love for Robin. *How am I to explain to my brother that I'm in love with his girl?*

How can I hide this from him? A.J.'s cell phone rang. He picked it up, thinking it was O.J. calling him back. "Hello?"

It was Dameon. "Aaron John O'Neil, I can't stop thinking of you. I want to see you."

"Dameon, I can't talk to you now. Please not now. I'll phone you later." He hung up the phone.

Robin had helped him to overcome his feelings for Dameon. Now Dameon wanted him back, but he was in love with Robin not Dameon. He felt like his emotions were on a rollercoaster. A.J. wanted a drink.

Westchester

Dameon went back to the table where Ellen was waiting. His attitude very curt after A.J. had hung up on him. Hurt and angry, he didn't care to be with anyone.

"Ellen, gather your things. We're leaving."

"Dameon, is there something wrong? Did I do something? Did something happen?"

Dameon was very short with her. "It's not you, it's me. Now let me take you to your car. I had a lovely time tonight."

Ellen was quiet on the drive back to Dameon's place. She figured he must have called his mystery woman, and they had a spat because he had a completely different attitude after making his phone call. Ellen was furious.

How dare she interrupt my evening with him? I'm going to find out who this big bitch is and confront her.

They arrived at Dameon's. He didn't invite her in. Ellen was upset. She had thought the evening was hers.

"Ellen, I apologize for my demeanor, but suddenly I'd like to spend the evening alone. Don't take it personally. I have a few problems I need to attend to."

"I understand, Dameon."

"Thanks for the date. Drive safely."

Ellen was frantic. She had to know who this person was who had so much power over the man she wanted. She made up her mind to hire a private detective, even though she had given Robin her word that she wouldn't. Dameon meant too much to her not to know who was getting all of his attention.

Florida

"A.J., tell me, how did it go? Did she believe you? Or should I say 'us'?"

"Yes, O.J., she bought it. I passed for you." A.J. was not happy about what he had done.

"Is there anything I should know, anything you need to fill me in on?" O.J. asked.

"No. She's a fine woman, and she loves the hell out of you."

O.J. grinned. "Man, I told you she's special."

"Let's change clothes. You don't want to keep her waiting."

They exchanged clothes. O.J. was nervous; the moment he had been waiting for had finally arrived. Once again he was going to see the woman who gave him life.

"A.J., I just want to tell you how much I appreciate what you've done for me." He hugged his brother and told him he loved him. "I love you man. You're the greatest. I gotta go now, but I'll get in touch with you when she leaves."

"OK, O.J., now go."

O.J. left as if he was going to a fire. A.J. poured a drink to calm his nerves. He was so saddened in spirit. He had let his guard down and allowed love to fill his heart. Emotions were running deep. Robin was everything he had dreamed a mate could be. How was he to deal with it? He didn't want to hurt his brother, but he didn't want to say good-bye to Robin either.

O.J. pulled up to the door of the beach house. Both his hands and knees were trembling because he was so nervous. He got out of the car, approached the door and fumbled to put the key in to open the door to the woman he loved. O.J. ran to Robin and picked her up off her feet. He held her tight in his arms and kissed her before he said a word to her.

"Robin, Robin, oh how I missed you so! I love you so much!" O.J. was kissing her on her neck and in the places that aroused them both.

Robin was confused. "O.J. what's wrong? You're acting like you're seeing me for the first time. I'm not complaining, but what's going on?"

O.J. said, "Baby, everything is fine." He picked her up, carried her to the bedroom, laid her across the bed and began to kiss her all over. They both got caught up in the heat of love.

"O.J. the test, what about the test?"

"It's over now. I want you. I need you. I got to have you!"

"Take me, O.J. I'm yours."

O.J. made love to her as if he hadn't been with a woman in years, gently stroking her with every ounce of love he had to give. There were no words spoken; their bodies did the talking. They both were in ecstasy as they made love for hours.

Westchester

Meanwhile, Dameon was an emotional wreck from A.J.'s putting him off. He thought his scheme of making A.J. think there was someone else would make him run back to him. Instead it was backfiring. Dameon had tried to fight the feelings he had for A.J. He had tried to move forward, but love stopped him. He was angry, yet saddened by their breakup. Dameon poured a glass of scotch, sat in his recliner and reflected back on his trip to Seattle.

Dameon knew A.J. couldn't go for long without him. They both shared a common denominator. The secret love affair they had shared for years. Dameon awaited A.J.'s call. Emotions spiraling downward, he needed to feel confident about himself. The only time he felt sure about himself was when he was dressed in elegance; the way A.J. adored seeing him. He went upstairs to the dressing room and pulled a shoulder-length blonde wig off the shelf. He began to put his makeup on, preparing his face as if he were in a beauty contest. Face beautifully made up, he slipped on his wig and looked at himself in the mirror.

He was ready to call A.J. again. Dameon had the confidence he needed. This time he was not going to be rejected. He was ready to tell A.J. how he felt, ready to express his love. Feeling very feminine gave him boldness, a power to conquer all roadblocks. Adoring himself in the mirror, he needed the appropriate outfit to complete his look.

He went to the closet and pulled out a purple and silver sequined dress, A.J.'s favorite. Dameon got dressed. Looking in the mirrors that surrounded the room, he was able to take a full look at himself. He was gorgeous.

Suddenly Dameon snapped. He hated what he saw in the mirror. He hated who he'd become. He took the glass of scotch and threw it at the mirror. The glass shattered everywhere. Dameon fell to his knees and broke down. A.J. had crushed his manhood, stolen his heart. Dameon lay weeping for hours.

Florida

"I'd like to inquire about two tickets previously purchased from Atlanta to Daytona tomorrow afternoon. Can you please help me?"

"Ma'am, I'm very sorry, but we cannot give out that information unless you were the one who purchased the tickets," the airport attendant said.

"Lady, look, my husband is flying in from Atlanta with a relative on your airline, and I need to know his flight number and time."

The attendant said, "If you will give me your husband's name, I can tell you his itinerary."

"Oscar James O'Neil is the name, and his brother's name is Aaron John O'Neil."

The attendant said, "Please hold, ma'am, while I look up the information."

Not only was Samone pissed off with the attendant, but she was feeling suspicious and wanted to check on O.J.

The attendant came back on the line. "I'm sorry, ma'am. We have no one by those names on our passenger list."

Samone said, "Thank you."

She was furious. She'd had a gut feeling that something wasn't right when O.J. was in such a hurry to get to A.J. She tried calling A.J.'s house to see if he answered the phone, but she got his answering machine. She knew the two of them were up to something. What it was she couldn't put her finger on.

Beach House

"Robin, I'm so glad you're here. Marry me. Be my wife."

"Are you serious, O.J.?"

"Yes, sweet Robin, I've never been so serious about anything in my life. I love you, and I'm sure I want to spend the rest of my life with you."

"Honey, of course I want to marry you. But let's not rush it. Shouldn't we spend more time together? Get to know each other's kids and families? O.J., I've never felt this way for anyone; it's almost frightening. Almost too good to be true. I guess I'm scared of losing what we have. I love you so much."

O.J. held Robin's face and looked her straight in the eyes and said, "Robin as long as there's breath in my body, and I'm able to function, you'll never have to worry about losing what we share. I want you in my future. I need you in my life. My days and nights are incomplete without you. I've found my happiness in you. I'm sure I want to make you my wife."

"Honey, I'm honored to be the future Mrs. O'Neil, but can we slow the pace down a little? At least get in one state? We both have our careers, the kids and the houses. We need to take it day by day and give it some time. I'm not going anywhere. We can travel back and forth until we finalize everything."

"Sweetheart, you're absolutely right. I realize things take time. It's just that I want you here with me all the time. Kiss me, Robin. How I've longed to be with you!"

They embraced each other in a long passionate kiss, both wrapped in a moment of love. O.J. forgot about Samone; all he wanted was Robin.

Westchester

"Hello, this is Got to Know Investigation Services. How may I direct your call?"

"Hello, my name is Ellen Berk. I'm in need of your service. I need your best P.I. available."

"Yes, Ms. Berk that would be Allen Kimble. He's our top man, very expensive, but very good at what he does."

"Cost is not an issue. Is Mr. Kimble available?"

"Ms. Berk, I'm sorry, but he's currently out working on a case. If you would please give me a number where you can be reached, I'll have him contact you just as soon as possible."

Dameon's Place

Dameon was passed out, lying on the floor when he heard the phone ringing in the distance. His voice was low and emotionally broken when he answered. "This is Dameon speaking."

It was Mark, the man who'd spoken to him at the restaurant. "Dameon, hi, it's Mark. We spoke at Lamarage. Are you busy tonight?"

Dameon pulled himself together, wiping off the makeup he had ruined with his tears. "Why, Mark, you're timing is impeccable. I'd love to meet with you. Shall we say 11 p.m. at the Grand Hotel?"

Mark said, "Great, I'll see you there."

Dameon was finished weeping over A.J. He needed to go on with his life. Maybe a date with Mark would help him overcome his feelings for A.J. *It's time to move on*, he thought. He got dressed to meet Mark.

Florida at A.J.'s Place

A.J. heard Samone's voice on the answering machine. He wanted so desperately to contact O.J. to let him know Samone was checking on him. He sat gazing at Robin's picture, imagining making love to her. He wanted so desperately to be in his brother's shoes. He needed to see her again, before she left Florida. But how? By now, A.J. was intoxicated. He drank his troubles away. With Robin's picture in his hand, he drifted off to sleep.

O.J. and Robin made love most of the night, but the day had arrived for them to part. Robin had to return home, and her flight was scheduled to leave at noon.

"Thank you, O.J., for three lovely days. I'm going to miss you so much."

"Robin, you know I was very serious about making you my wife."

"Yes, honey. I'm serious too. I can't wait for you to meet my family. I'll plan a dinner party for next month so you can meet everyone."

"Perfect. We can get engaged and tell everyone the news. Robin, you mean so much to me. I love you very much."

"I love you too, O.J., and I'd be honored to be your wife."

A.J. awoke with Robin's picture in his hand. He looked at his watch; it was 10:45. He had time to freshen up and get to the airport to see her off. A.J. planned to hide in the distance to see Robin one last time. He had to see the woman who had opened his heart to love. Half the night he had battled with the idea of confronting his brother with his feelings for Robin.

A.J. didn't want to hurt his brother, but for the first time in years, he was sure of what he wanted. He knew he had to have Robin. He wanted to tell O.J. everything about his past relationships, including the long affair he'd had with Dameon. He wanted the truth to be known about why he had never married, why he had all those beautiful models on his arm as a cover-up for the lifestyle he was living. Finally he was ready to give up all the masquerading for Robin. He felt that this was a peace ground discussion.

Robin and O.J. were saying their good-byes at the airport. A.J., disguised in a trench coat off in the distance, looked on as his brother kissed the woman who had stolen his heart. A.J. walked away, head hung down, feeling crushed and heartbroken. He had to confront O.J. tonight before they compared details of spending time with Robin. A.J. walked away and drove off to peace ground.

"Sweetheart, call me as soon as you walk in the door."

Teary-eyed, Robin said, "I promise to call, O.J. Thanks for loving me."

O.J. removed a hankie from his jacket pocket to wipe her tears. "Robin," he said, "now there will be no tears. I promise you I'll see you very soon, and once you become my wife, we'll never have to worry about parting again, until death do us part."

They kissed and said their good-byes. Robin walked toward her plane, not once looking back. O.J. stood there looking as if he lost everything he ever had in the world.

O.J. headed for his car. He opened the door, and on the seat lay a white rose Robin had left with a note. The note read: "My love for you will stand. I'll let nothing separate me from your love until we're together again. Always and forever loving you. Remember someone on the opposite side lives, cares and thinks of you. Thank you for a lovely weekend, Robin."

A.J. looked at his watch. Robin's plane was in the air. She was gone, on her way home. *I let the love of my life get away*, he thought. He called O.J. on his cell phone to arrange for him to meet with him at peace ground. O.J.'s voice mail picked up.

"O.J., it's very urgent that you meet me at peace ground at two o'clock. I need to talk to you. I'll be waiting."

O.J. hadn't checked his calls. He was feeling rather lonely and down – missing Robin so much already. He thought he'd go to peace ground to sort out his feelings, not even aware that A.J. was there as well.

Peace Ground

A.J. was sitting on the railing of the building overlooking the view, contemplating how to explain to his brother his love for Robin. Thinking about how close he and O.J had been all their lives, he didn't want to lose the closeness. They were bonded at birth, yet A.J. had kept part of his life hidden. Now he was ready to come clean, tell O.J. everything, including what he felt for Robin. A.J.'s back was turned towards the city; he didn't see his brother approaching.

"A.J. hey what's up? What brings you to peace ground this time of day? Did we have a meeting?"

"I guess it's ironic we both end up here to sort out our thoughts. In fact, I did call and left a message for you to meet me here at 2 p.m."

"Man, A.J. what's going on? You looked deep in thought as I came up."

Loretta Heard

"Guess we both have something on our minds. O.J., you know you're the closet person to me, and we've always been able to discuss everything."

O.J. said, "I know that, bro. I want to thank you for helping me. There's something I need to tell you before I tell anyone else."

"O.J., before you say anything, I've got something to tell you, too."

"Speak to me, A.J. Tell me what's on your mind."

"For years I've kept part of my life from you and the world. I'm not the person you think I am. Sure, we're brothers, but there are things about me you don't know about," A.J. tested the waters.

"What are you talking about, A.J.?"

"Well you've often questioned me about marriage and kids, and as you know, that was a subject I've always avoided. Do you want to know why? (Pause) Because I dated both men and women. O.J., I was searching for my sexuality."

"What are you saying A.J.? You were bisexual? What about all those beautiful women?"

294

"They were friends -- really cover-ups for me. For years I've been seriously involved with a man named Dameon."

O.J. looked at his brother with amazement. "A.J., listen, you're my brother, and your personal life is your business. I love you unconditionally. Whatever makes you happy makes me happy. I'd never think any less of you. Why would you keep this from me?"

A.J. said, "For years I wanted to share this with you, but up until today, I saw no reason to."

"A.J. why are you dropping this on me now?" O.J. interrupted but wouldn't let A.J. answer the question.

"No matter what you're doing, A.J. I love you, bro. (Pause) Hey, wait, now let me share my news. It's almost as big a bombshell as yours! I asked Robin to be my wife, and I owe it all to you. You made me realize how much of my own life I've lost out on."

A.J.'s face grew angry. He said, "O.J., you asked me why I am sharing my bisexuality with you now – today? I'll tell you. Because of Robin. I've fallen in love with her."

Both of them were face to face.

"Now wait a minute, A.J. She's my girl. I'm in love with Robin. She's going to be my wife. I'm sorry, my brother, but I was there first," O.J. said adamantly.

A.J. didn't say a word. Before he knew it, he had taken a swing at O.J. They began to fight. Tossing hits back and forth, they forgot they were on the roof of the building. Suddenly one of them lost his balance, slipped and fell over the rail.

Sequel to come

in Book II

Loretta Heard

About the Author

She's an aspiring new author with an imagination to share.

Printed in the United States
20957LVS00004B/24